a novel

Jackytar

douglas gosse

Douglas Gosse (signature)

JESPERSON PUBLISHING

JESPERSON PUBLISHING
100 Water Street   P.O. Box 2188
St. John's   NL   Canada   A1C 6E6

Library and Archives Canada Cataloguing in Publication

Gosse, Douglas, 1966-
        Jackytar / Douglas Gosse.

ISBN 1-894377-13-3

I. Title.

PS8563.O83695J33 2005   C813'.54   C2005-900805-9

Cover & Interior Design: Rhonda Molloy
Editor: Tamara Reynish

Printed in Canada.

Contents

Foreward

This is a work of fiction with one notable exception. Rev. Dr. Brent Hawkes, a prominent social activist and pastor of the Metropolitan Community Church of Toronto (MCCT), is very much real. Several times throughout the novel, I refer to Rev. Dr. Brent Hawkes, his sermons and MCCT as if the protagonist, Alex, were a member of that congregation. Other than that, all characters and situations are from my imagination and tacit knowledge. No other resemblance to actual persons living or dead is intended. I have tried to create a plausible reality that troubles readers to rethink social beliefs, customs and practices.

Author's *Note*

Dear Readers,

For a long time after I finished this book, I didn't move. I sat there, immobile, staring at my computer. Slowly, I moved my head, my hands and then I stood up and shook my legs. I walked out to the kitchen and poured myself a glass of cold water from the jug in the fridge. I gulped it down and it felt good. You see, last year, my mother, France Murphy, who was French-speaking and Native-White, or what some Newfoundlanders call a Jackytar, suddenly fell ill. I returned home to Bond Cove, Newfoundland, where I was born and bred, to be at her bedside in her last days and lend support to my family. I was home, all total, for about one week. During this time, I had my laptop computer with me and wrote in my journal. It was one of the most trying periods of my life. Confronting the past is never easy. Nor is breaking silences. And there were many in my life to be broken. Silent spectres from the past that haunted me. This I realised more and more as the weeks wore on, following my return to Toronto. So I used my journal entries to construct the following story. What we Newfoundlanders call a yarn. Be they glimpses or insights into my experiences, as you read, I hope you, too, may confront some of your silences and attempt to break them.

Sincerely,

Alex Murphy

Pre*lude*

"I'll just be a few minutes, okay?"

"Ya need some help?"

"No, I know where it's all at."

"Ya sure?"

"Yeah, don't worry. Be back in a few minutes. I'll do it."

He appeared satisfied. "I'll check the ile and clean out the car a bit then. Make sure she's ready."

She entered the house, furtively glancing behind her at the passengers in the waiting car. No one followed. The hallway seemed endless. She idly tried the door but it was locked, of course. The stairs were carpeted and the steps wide, but she paused to contemplate them. She knew she had to climb and quickly, so she gripped the rail, afraid of falling and began her ascent. At the top, chest heaving, she felt dizzy. She stopped a moment to regain her composure.

"No time!" she cursed.

The bedroom door opened soundlessly. The key hung

on a hook inside the walk-in closet. She grabbed it and put it in her pocket. She glanced at all the clothes. Clothes that might never be worn again. This was a house of death. She stuffed several items into a carry-on bag: forgotten nightgowns, more underwear and a few extra toiletries from the dresser and washroom. All a premise to get the key and accomplish her mission. She looked at her watch.

At the top of the flight of stairs, she shrugged. An idle thought occurred to her, as was often the case these days.

"What goes up, must come down!"

She rushed back down the stairs, almost slipping midway, but she caught herself by grabbing onto the railing. She turned the key in the lock. The door opened with the tiniest creak. She stopped, paralysed, and held her breath. All she heard was the ticking of the grandfather clock in the hallway. Julian. Evidence of him all around the house, in the polished floors and the crisply painted walls, even at the threshold of the sanctuary where his presence was so conspicuously absent and therefore everywhere. Quickly, she entered, closed the door and leaned against it.

The room seemed slightly sinister to her. The beige walls closed in. The stained glass panes of the *oeil de bœuf* window permitted only meagre light to sift through. Yet, she didn't dare turn on a lamp. One of them in the car might take notice and the jig'd be up. She glanced at the music books lined up on the shelves, the photographs, the Edwardian table, and bolstered her resolve.

She had a job to do and that was that!

She rushed across the small room. The excitement of the day was almost too great for her. She felt dizzy again and steadied herself on the pump organ until the lights stopped exploding in her head.

No time to waste!

Her eyes settled on the adjacent steamer trunk. She lifted the cherub dolls off the elaborate doily, placed them behind the trunk and draped the doily over the armchair. Then she retrieved the key from its hiding place on a ledge underneath the organ lid. She unlocked the trunk. No time for tiredness now. She took the music scores out and laid them on the floor. Next, the black leather case. She opened it. Inside were neat rows of tapes. She donned her glasses and peered at the dates, using her finger to read down the rows. There were many, some dating back five years, most from the past two years. Which one. She couldn't recall exactly. She lifted out the top deck, satisfied that it wasn't there. She repeated the process for the bottom layer.

Finally, there it was, *Témoignage* written across the side.

Quickly, she took it out and opened the case. Empty! She panicked and began searching frantically among the other tapes and contents of the trunk. Nowhere to be found. She mumbled a prayer as she searched.

"Please St. Anthony, come around. Something's lost and can't be found."

Time was running out.

"Ya awright?"

Her heart leapt into her throat. She couldn't stop now. She stood still until the heart palpitations subsided. Then she realized the voice was coming from the porch. He couldn't see where she was coming from. Tentatively, she opened the door and peeked outside. The coast was clear.

"Oh just grand!" she responded in a carefully casual tone.

She walked towards the porch where he stood leaning

Jackytar

against the doorsill. She handed him the suitcase. "Here. I'll be another minute. Gotta go to the washroom," she added apologetically. "Stomach problems. That time of the month," she said lightly.

He blushed and turned away. "Okay, sure. Take yer time. No rush."

She couldn't believe she had just said that. She closed the door behind her, raced to the sanctuary and put everything back in order, lickety-split. Dizziness or not, she had to go back up the stairs again and hang up the key. There was no two ways about it. A couple of minutes later, she descended, sweat gleaming on her brow.

He was waiting at the bottom.

"Ya awright?" he asked again.

"Yup. A bit of an upset stomach. Sorry to keep ya waiting."

She inhaled and scurried out the door, not glancing back for ghosts this time. She must have destroyed it and forgotten, she told herself. All the ghosts were on that tape, never to be seen or heard of again. No one else could have stolen it, could they? There was nothing she could do about it now. Another thought entered her head and she muttered it to herself as she departed.

"Hear no evil, see no evil."

one

■

Satur*day*

Le soleil s'est couché tôt aujourd'hui. I laid the novel on the
end table, stood and peered out over the view of
downtown Toronto. Yellow and white lights from inside
brightened some of the apartments. I imagined happy
scenes in some. Less happy in others, especially the low
income housing just a few blocks away that might as well
have been another universe. I used to live in such
buildings. Lots of nice people but crazy people, too.
Desperate people. And cheap parquet flooring. Dingy walls
so that the next tenants could move in and not be shocked
by colour. Shared laundry rooms where you had to guard
your clothes like a hawk. I was glad to be away from all
that. The houses below looked dark and empty. Those
people worked late. The autumn days were increasingly
grey but I liked the soothing gloom. I dreamt of snow.
Crisp snow to end the interminable autumn, so that
downhill skiing could resume and maybe Keith would
return to his old self.

I ambled into the bathroom and swiped at a moth. Slow, stupid creatures. It fell to the floor. There were no screens on the patio doors or windows when we moved in, so moths had invaded our closets and attacked our fluffy bathroom towels. I blew my nose. Startlingly red blood speckled the white tissue. The air was so dry with the heating system on. I blew my nose hard. Again. And again. Then threw the bloody tissue into the toilet and flushed so I wouldn't have to empty the waste paper basket every hour.

Noise.

A knock at the door?

No one ever knocked. We lived in a security building. I hadn't buzzed anyone in and it couldn't have been a neighbour. We staunchly avoided one another. The unwritten code. Downtown Toronto was an oasis for earning dirty lucre. Condo *community* living was a joke, a market ploy, unless you wanted to call work-obsessed people of a certain age and salary range who detested interacting with one another a community. After a day of ferocious competition and feigned outward civility, seeing ourselves mirrored in each other's fatigued eyes, expensive haircuts and fancy clothes was too painful for most to bear. Even in the elevator. Ignore the neighbours.

The artifice of it. The futility. No energy left to carry on *The Pleasant Charade*. Sudden alarm. Bad news, a fire, a heart attack, a mutant moth invasion? The knocking resumed. Could Keith have been injured?

I rushed to the door and swung it open.

"Hey, how are ya, Alex? I left my keys with Corey. He's still at the club. Cell phone off. Or he can't hear me with the music. Me and the boys are gonna come hang out for a while."

It was Keith.

DOUGLAS GOSSE

Corey, a twenty year-old twink who couldn't hold a fulltime job, was Keith's flavour of the month. I was glad he hadn't come along, but little comfort that was. Three sketchy men hid behind Keith. They bore a similar look. The look of having been up all night. Tousled hair and rumpled clothes. The stink of smoke and beer. Vacant eyes from drugs that hadn't yet worn off. Keith, however, looked delightfully healthy despite the reddened eyes and needing a shower. Good genes and daily workouts at the gym seemed to be keeping him fit for the time being, but I wondered how long he could keep it up.

I didn't respond, at least not verbally, but I noted with satisfaction that the bottom lip of the prissy little queen with the tight shirt trembled.

"Alex, this is Greg, Ed and Carlos," Keith said.

Little circular orbs in the ceiling, placed vertically at three and a half foot intervals, on a dimmer switch, created an intimate atmosphere. They walked in self-consciously, like gangly adolescents who happened to be in their twenties and thirties but forgot. Lucky for them, they removed their shoes. I had just finished cleaning an hour ago. The floors were immaculate, swept and mopped, glistening even with the soft overhead lights. A lemony scent hovered in the air.

The furniture gleamed. Not one thing was out of place. No magazines dangled from end tables or from the joined sofa and love seat. No glasses or mugs marred the pristine patina of the leather coffee table. A specialist in Yorkville had designed the cloth blinds for the sliding glass doors in the living room. Beige with horizontal chocolate stripes intended to broaden the feel of the room. All Keith's doing. The furnishings were meant to impress. But they were uncomfortable.

Jackytar

"Wow! This condo is really something!" admired Carlos. Or Greg. Or Ed.

"Nice, huh," said Keith. "We bought it two years ago this January. Just throw your coats on the sofa and I'll show you around."

"I'll be in the bedroom," I sputtered to Keith.

I couldn't breathe. I grabbed a few tissues, blew my nose again and threw the bloody remains in the black waste paper basket. I plonked myself down on the stark white comforter and held my head in my hands. I had decorated the bedroom to my personal taste. Postmodernist décor. We each had a separate bedroom. Only I used the den as an office. I listened to their muffled voices. Ohhs and ahhs as Keith showed off the place. His place, really, bought with money he earned as an accountant on Bay Street.

"Hey, what's up?" Keith peered into the bedroom. "Are you mad at me?"

"Yes, I'm mad. Where the hell were you again all night and day?"

He came into the bedroom and sat beside me. It was impossible to gauge his expression. The glossy eyes and monotone voice made him inscrutable.

"Ya know I went out with the boys. It was Friday night! We had some fun."

"You have a cell phone. You could've called. It's Saturday evening! What a tired story. And one I'm sick of hearing!"

"Huh? Whattaya mean? I don't get it."

"I'm tired of this shit!" His red eyes widened. "You going out and not returning for twenty-four or forty-eight hours. Coming home with street trash."

DOUGLAS GOSSE

It took him a moment to process. "Hey, I'm entitled to my fun. I work hard. I need to unwind."

"Unwind? Are you out of your mind? How do you call doing party drugs and dancing for sixteen hours straight with strangers, unwinding? You don't even know these…people." I nodded towards the living room, where Greg or Ed or Carlos had put music on the stereo. Boom. Boom. Boom.

"Keith, they could be thieves or killers for all we know. And you bring them here, to our home! Where'd you find them this time?"

"That's your opinion, I guess. We met at the Underground. They're nice guys. One's a cop. One's a nurse. The other guy works in a shop, I think. Now why don't ya just come out and mingle? It might be fun. We used to have fun, don't you remember?"

He almost managed a charming grin. Then lost it faster than a straight guy checking out another guy on the sidewalk. He had no real passion for generating charm, irony, sarcasm, anger, or any emotion anymore.

"If you think I'm going to go out there and mingle with those losers, you're delusional. You can't even hold a sensible conversation with them. They're zoned out. Forget it. I have better things to do."

He got up and walked quietly to the door. Turned around. He was about to add something when my cell phone rang. I quickly blew my nose again and tossed the bloody tissue away before answering. For some reason, the knot in my stomach worsened.

"What is it?" Keith asked once I'd hung up.

"I have to go back. Tonight. She's dying."

Jackytar

t w o

■

CN Tower

on the highest peak of the world
I trod with trepidation
a glass floor threatened to swallow me
send me careening to the ground below
you said it was safe
and together we walked on clouds

the lights of the city left me bewildered
I didn't know which way to look
so beautiful, blinking yellow and white
blinding stringed lanterns on streets
and the blazing beam of your smile

I held you briefly in my hands,
a sun of golden radiance,
and felt a little closer
to infinity

three

■

"Well, now, looky who we got here!" sang Jeremy.

"Whatcha doin today?" asked Sandra, her voice syrupy.

"Just gettin some stuff at the shop," said Alex.

"What? Tampons?" said Jeremy.

Sandra snickered.

"Ya got a pussy in those jeans, Alex?" said Austin, their cousin, a teenager a few years older, stocky and strong from working in the local lumber mill. Alex commanded his legs to move but they felt like jelly. He tried to remain expressionless.

On répond aux imbéciles par le silence.

A rough hand fastened on his shoulder. "Hey, I was talkin to ya!"

"Ya fancies un, don't ya Austin? Maybe ya wants to date un, eh?" Sandra said. "Take un ap in the alders then and have some fun!"

The redness spread from Alex's ears down to his neck.

"No fuckin way!"

"Whatcha holdin onto his shoulder for then?" Sandra sneered. "Luh, he's in heat. All flushed like a bitch. Go fer it, Austin."

Austin let go of his shoulder like he had leprosy. Then he spat on the dusty road and stepped back. "Goddamn gay pussy faggot!"

"Ah, now you'm hurtin his feelins. Leave Alex alone, youse. He's m'friend. Ain't ya Alex?" Jeremy grabbed him by the arm and tried to kiss his face. "Wanna play hoist-yer-sails-and-run wid us?

Sandra and Austin pretended to gag.

"Watch out! Ya might catch AIDS," Sandra said.

"Let's git the fuck outta here," Austin said. "Leave the little Jackytar pussy alone."

"O'revwraaar!" drawled Sandra.

They sauntered off, giggling.

The boy walked alone. Past saltbox houses. He looked at the landwash. Remembered having spent time there with Sandra two years ago when they were ten years old. They had poked at a gigantic cobweb. The biggest spider they'd ever seen scurried away from their sticks. Sandra had toyed with the spider until she got fed up and squished it with her stick. He'd hidden his squeamishness from her. Voicing it might have risked her friendship.

Not that it mattered anymore.

He thought about Nanny. Every morning, she used to have toast and tea ready for him at the kitchen table, overlooking the bay. Toast cooked over the wood stove and real butter. Delicious hort jam, what some called blueberry, picked on the Bond Cove barrens. He missed her. The Atlantic Ocean used to look so peaceful from the kitchen window. Now it just reminded him that he had to escape, that somewhere out there he might find happiness. And be safer.

"Why do things have to change?" he muttered aloud.

He spied Ole Man Howell working in his garden, using an old-fashioned sickle to cut the grass like in the olden days. He faked a smile and waved. Someone was always watching. Except when he needed them most. Through parted curtains. From a shed. From a passing car. This was an old people's town. Young people moved to the Mainland to get jobs – Toronto or Fort McMurray.

To escape, maybe like he had to. One way or another.

He walked along Brigg's Road. The curving dirt road hugged the ocean. The houses were pretty colours. Red. Blue. White. Beige. Red was his favourite. Especially the faded red of Johnson General Store. Boarded up now for years. He remembered shopping there as a small boy with his Nanny and Poppy. Mannequins loomed overhead, and more than once, he could have sworn their limbs stirred or a head cocked slightly in his direction.

"Git some candy popcorn, m'ducky, if ya wants," she used to say.

Once, his Poppy Murphy had called him over for a special gift.

"Look, m'son, let's git ya some t'igh rubbers, awright?"

Poppy did indeed buy him thigh rubbers and he had worn them proudly that whole evening, until bed.

"Ya gotta go to sleep, now," Poppy cooed. "Wear em for just anot'er little while."

But he had never really enjoyed trouting. Poppy would have liked spending more time with him trouting in silence on the ponds and sometimes spinning yarns. He

Jackytar

enjoyed the yarns, but trouting was boring. And he hated it when Poppy Murphy killed a trout.

"What's the matter, b'y?" Poppy Murphy had asked him the first time. "That don't hurt em none, luh!"

And he'd bashed the struggling trout's head against a rock to prove his point and then tossed it in the basket. "Trout don't feel not'in a t'all!"

But he'd always suspected that trout did feel pain. And he couldn't bring isself to do it. Eventually, his grandfather stopped coaxing him along.

And he didn't like the rough softball games in on the field either. The older boys swore. They grabbed each other by the bum or balls. They talked dirty about girls. And that always made him feel ashamed. The younger boys strove to copy them. But not him.

"What's wrong? You idden a girl, is ya?"

"You should go play wid the girls' team!"

Or sugar sweet tones. "Leave un alone. He's m'buddy. Alex prefers the books. Right Alex? You idden into the girls yet, is ya? I can't blame ya. No time for that when ya gotta study, right?"

More often than not, he'd try to laugh it off, or ignore it, hoping it'd go away. His mother had taught him, "*On répond aux imbéciles par le silence!*"

One by one, most of his local friends started imitating the older boys. This past summer had been agony, even though he had a couple of friends visiting from Ottawa and a few other outsiders who still chose to hang out with him. Alex thought about crossing Jeremy, Sandra and Austin Smith for the hundredth time.

He wished he had no feelings like the trout.

Being treated like he was a piece of shit hurt deep

down and there was physical pain. He stopped and held his stomach for a moment. There was only so much he could take. Funny how they never went after him when they were alone. Never when he was with his few remaining friends. Just when he was outnumbered.

The past two weeks in Bond Cove had been pure torture.

How he loved Shepherd's Bluff, where away from the others, he felt safe. He used to love hearing about the pirate legends from Poppy Murphy, but Poppy told him he was getting too old for that now. He still spent hours wandering the mossy footpaths, conscious of the blue bay and its small boats sailing in and out, day after day. He heard sheep close by and was mindful not to step in dung. Just last summer, he had spent hours here playing space warriors with friends. Now most of them avoided him like the plague and joined the likes of Sandra, Austin and Jeremy Smith. Drinking and getting into mischief started early in Bond Cove. He crouched down almost flat, feet first, and slid over the edge of the cliff. Rocks and pebbles rolled to the bottom, but he wasn't afraid. He'd climbed down this same drang tons of times.

At the bottom, he sat on the rock.

"My Rock," he thought. Shaped like a chair with armrests. Facing the Atlantic Ocean. Despite it being summertime, the wind felt chilly. His bum grew numb on the icy seat.

"I hate being called Jackytar. I hate being made fun of because I speak French! Oi'm not a lazy half-breed Indian! I'm not a faggot!" he said aloud, starting to weep. "I hate my life!"

Jackytar

He reached down and gingerly picked up a piece of broken beer bottle. He twisted the amber glass back and forth. The sun was bright but he was seated in shadows. Alone. Miserable. He pressed the shard to his wrist…

Déclic!

"Excuse me sir, would you like a snack?"

I heard metallic sounds: clicking seatbelts and clanging utensils. "Pardon?" I said, waking up and opening my eyes.

"Would you like a snack? Perhaps some bottled water? A soft drink?"

I removed my hand from my wrist where the tiny scar remained and recalled bits and pieces of the dream I'd just had. Memories to be more precise. My mouth felt dry and gritty.

"Yes, some water, please."

"Then please put your laptop away. I'll be back shortly."

The flight attendant, an athletic man with a narrow waist and broad shoulders, worked his way down the aisle, serving right and left. I pressed a button and my seat righted itself. The interior of the plane was bathed in gentle grey shadows. I put my laptop in its case and stored it underneath my seat. The flight attendant returned and handed me bottled water, a glass and a napkin.

"Are you from here?" he asked.

"Huh?"

"You just visiting?"

"I'm originally from Newfoundland but now I live in Toronto. How long until we land?"

"Oh won't be too long now. We left Montreal a few minutes ago and you fell asleep like a baby. Maybe another hour and a bit? We have the winds behind our sails as the Capt'n says. Excited?"

"Yeah, it's been a few years."

"Well, nothing ever changes on the Rock!"

I smiled but the knot in my stomach worsened.

Jackytar

f o u r

■

After midnight or early morning. I arrived at a transition place. Limbo. The word *displacement* entered my consciousness. Disjointed, fluid, like a meandering soul with glowing tentacles, I imagined, flowing from Newfoundland to Quebec to Toronto. I lingered somewhere out there. Over the Atlantic Ocean. In the damp fog above the stormy sea. Isolation. Not myself. Someone different. Neither here nor there.

I looked around. At all the light haired people. So different from Toronto. The smiling and tired people. A father carried a child in his arms. The mother tried to grab a suitcase but wasn't quick enough. It sailed on by. She stuck her lip out and gave her husband a dirty look. He raised his eyebrows and looked toward the slumbering child of two or three nestled in his arms, then at her. She turned away and resumed her task. The luggage won't get by her next time.

The carousel went round and round. Many people had

left. I glanced outside the glass windows. I was in a cage. Or were they, outside, in the cage?

Still no sign of the brother.

The laptop case on my shoulder felt heavy. I switched shoulders. I considered asking the luggage claim person in the corner for assistance. But then the medium-size backpack chugged out through the flapped opening. A matching set of beige leather luggage trailed behind it. An overweight man grabbed it, huffing with the exertion. He put it on a trolley, but crashed into the carousel as he tried to manoeuvre. He pulled away and wheeled it ahead of me.

I had bought the backpack last summer for my trip to France. *La patrie.* It still looked new and fresh, untarnished. Navy blue and silky to my touch, belying its toughness. I had dragged it north and south, east and west, from the Atlantic Ocean of *la Bretagne* to the soothingly warm Mediterranean on the *Côte d'Azur.*

I took the backpack and slung it over my shoulders with a practised motion. It wasn't heavy but a part of me. The automatic doors opened. I looked around. The fat man had gone. There was no one to greet me. Several stragglers lingered. They looked lost. Bizarre in this antiseptic environment. Dishevelled. Free floating. Out of place. One looked to be little more than a child. A teenager of fifteen or sixteen. They seemed to be guarding their belongings. Dispassionately looking forward.

Waiting.

I walked up and down the airport. A few employees were working behind their desks. No one glanced up. He was nowhere to be seen.

I debated calling: Perhaps I should get a cab? Check in

Jackytar

at a hotel near the hospital?

Instead, I sat near the main entrance. And waited, becoming one of the lost. The minutes ticked by on the chrome wall clock. The metallic garbage can and plastic chairs shone. A solitary janitor pushed a mop across a section of floor. Over and over. Until it glistened and I was sure it could get no brighter. She wore an intent expression on her face.

Neat as a pin.

Her house must be neat as a pin.

At twenty-seven minutes past midnight, he entered. Fair haired and moustached, looking like a young Viking. He spotted me at the same moment I spotted him. A slight tremor on his lip as he neared me, his gait purposeful.

He said: How ya doin?

I said: I'm fine. Tired, but fine.

We headed out to his car. Not a car. A huge truck. Big wheels. Bright red, I was sure, in the daylight.

He started the truck.

I thanked him for picking me up. I didn't mention the wait.

I said: How's Maman?

He started the wipers. "Not well. The tumour is probably terminal. Doubt they can operate, but we'll find out soon for sure. She won't last long."

The dashboard glowed with eerie green light. Like a cockpit.

I said: Conscious?

Driftin in and out.

I said: For how long?

Few days.

I hesitated: Why didn't you call me earlier?

DOUGLAS GOSSE

He said: We wanted to be sure. It was sudden.

I looked for the trees. I couldn't see them but knew they were spruce, poplar, fir, and pine. Some birch. I had that familiar anticipation in my gut as I neared the Arterial Road. My old school.

Five years of my life. Teaching. Learning. Struggle. Victory. Growth. Oppression. Don't forget the oppression. The deafening silences. The smirks. The undercurrents of disdain.

Monsieur Alexandre — professeur extraordinaire / tapette, selon celui or celle à qui tu demandes. In so many words.

The school was bathed in spotlights. The grounds must be, too, but I couldn't see them. This was new. A security measure.

We journeyed forth over the road, past the Avalon Mall. Past clapboard houses. There were almost no brick houses here. We turned left towards downtown.

How nice, I thought. These Victorian houses. These charming dwellings. Had my brother and Evelyn purchased one of these?

I said: How are you doing? And Dad? How's he coping?

He said: Awright, I spose. Tough on the family. Unexpected. She babbles when she wakes up. Can't make much sense out of her. You might not recognize her. She's not like she was the last time ya seen her. Changed. Changed.

I said: And Evelyn?

The wife's okay, I spose.

I said: Oh.

In my head I thought: She was always her best during the holidays. Childlike. The music and carols and church

Jackytar

services seemed to fill her with joy. Animate her. The changes would start early November. The moroseness would leave her day-by-day like a leaky bucket. A light would begin to engulf her. The Christmas music was cathartic. The snow confirmed her faith in the magic of Christmas. In purity. Then, when Christmas Day was over, the opposite occurred. Like a balloon deflating. Little by little she would retreat.

He asked: How's the work goin?

His eyes were circled in black. I could smell the coffee.

I said: It's okay. Busy. But okay.

We arrived at the house. Victorian as I'd guessed. Three stories. Painted red. Like Johnson General Store. Some kind of light trim that was indistinguishable in the night.

Le soir tout les chats sont gris.

I heard a buzz. Perhaps from the power lines. I unloaded my backpack and crept inside, careful not to wake Evelyn and Dad. So still I could hear myself breathe. Our footsteps echoed on the polished floorboards. Bruce took my coat and hung it with his in the closet.

He said: She's been at the hospital non-stop since Friday. And she worked all week. Evelyn, I mean.

The porch smelled like pine. There were a few Christmas ornaments in the hallway. Already! Little Santa dolls and candles encased in fake leaves and berries perched on the shelf. A statue of the Virgin Mary with infant Jesus in arms adorned the far table. I wasn't used to ornamentation anymore. My condo was devoid of such things. Minimalist.

He said: Come this way. You're sleepin downstairs in the television room. Dad's in the guest room. Try not to wake un. He's bone tired. Just got home a while ago. Wore out. Been tendin to her day and night.

He showed me the way. The stairs were narrow and steep. These old houses. But everything had been renovated, fresh and new. Watercolours on the walls. Evelyn's touch. When he crossed in front of the closed door of the guest room, he put his index finger to his lips. Dad snored through the wall.

We entered the television room and he turned on the light. It was a large room. Overstuffed sofa. An entertainment system covered one wall. Machines for watching movies and listening to music. Rows of movies and a music collection. Pictures of the smiling married couple on every surface and bare wall; next to a weeping willow in Bannerman Park, leaning over a bridge above a gurgling brook and smearing cake on their faces at the reception. A more recent picture of them on vacation somewhere hot. Evelyn and Bruce had put on weight since their marriage. She wasn't waiflike anymore and she looked better. Bruce no longer had the physique of an elite athlete. His waist had thickened but his shoulders remained as broad as a hockey player's. His face seemed a bit puffy. A rollaway cot was made up for me in the corner.

He said: Are ya hungry?

He looked startled to have thought of my hunger.

No thank you, I lied. Really.

He appeared unsure, but started walking towards the door. Someone must have made him promise to see to my hunger.

Dad.

He said: G'night, then. We'll leave around 8:30 a.m. See ya in the marnin.

I bid him good night and thanked him again for

Jackytar

picking me up at the airport. He left. The stairs creaked. I heard some shuffling around upstairs. Then all was quiet. I could hear a pin drop.

I had to go to the washroom, but I didn't want to wake them, especially my father. I peed as quietly as possible, sitting on the toilet seat and then brushed my teeth with a mere drop of tap water. I didn't even flush the toilet. I cleaned my face with toner on a cotton pad, instead of water, crept back into the television room and closed the door softly.

I unpacked my clothes and put them in a neat pile on the floor next to the cot. I draped my good clothes over a chair. I took my laptop out of the case and booted it up. And wrote. The muffled click of the keys under my fingers. I imagined in the darkness, in the grey-green glow of my laptop, like a fairy glow. I imagined how she must be. Or not be. The void. The turmoil. The confusion. The pain?

Finally, I decided to call Keith, but he wasn't home. Images of bright strobe lights, shirtless men, loud music, and groping on a dance floor. I left a message, trying not to sound curt. Or too vulnerable. Or too needy. Or worried. But I was all of these things.

The flight was fine. Be careful. Call soon.

A light drizzle began falling. I looked out the window but there was no sea from this vantage point, only still houses and an occasional car.

C'est dur!

I swallowed the impulse to call Keith again. He wouldn't be home. And I'd feel – I didn't know what I'd feel. I lay on the cot and said my prayer:

f i v e

■

Our Fa…creator who art in heaven,
Hallowed be thy name;
Thy king…dominion come;
Thy will be done on earth as it is in heaven.
Give us this day our daily bread;
And forgive us our debts,
As we forgive our debtors.
And lead us not into temptation, but deliver us from evil;
For thine is the ki…dominion,
And the power and the glory,
For ever. Amen.

s i x

■

Sun*day*

That morning I awoke feeling tired and confused. I struggled out of bed and looked around at my new surroundings. A small framed picture caught my eye. Maman in profile playing the organ at St. Stephen's church in Bond Cove. There were Christmas decorations in the background. I used to accompany Maman to the church sometimes when I was a child. Aunt Flo, the official church organist, would only allow Maman to practice ever so often, usually upon the promptings of the minister who took pity on her. So she'd content herself at home playing hymns, especially music by Johann Sebastian Bach, whom she adored.

And I did, too.

"C'est le meilleur compositeur au monde, lui! Il n'y a pas mieux que lui, je te le dis!" she'd insist.

I'd nod my head, not quite sure whom she was talking about when I was a boy, but greatly impressed by the spirit of her conviction. Aunt Flo would call at the last minute only, as if the heavens and seas had suddenly parted and she were doing Maman a great favour.

Maman would drop whatever she was doing, throw on her jacket and fasten her boots, all in a flurry. The ring of the telephone and the noise down below would be the signal. The two of us would dart down Murphy's Hill making a beeline for St. Stephen's steeple. Her mastering of a musical piece often took months of intermittent practice, but she never relented until she got it to her satisfaction. When we entered, my mother would curtsey in the aisle, as they did in Roman Catholic churches. She taught me to bend on one knee and cross myself like the Roman Catholic men and boys. Micks, they called them, the Catholics. Twas a dirty word, I knowed, but I didn't want to displease her so I went along. We even crossed ourselves, too, until Aunt Flo peeked out from the vestry one day and caught us in the act.

"France, maid, I didn't realize you still did thaaat," she commented, drawing out the final word as if it were distasteful, over-enunciating, as was her trademark. "And in an Aaanglican chuuurch, tooo? My, how straaange tis indeeed. One really doesn't see thaaat often nooow, does one?"

Maman had turned bright red, lowered her eyes and remained silent. Aunt Flo turned on her heel but before she marched back into the vestry, she added insult to injury, "Pleeease wash your hands before you plaay, Fraance. The last time the keyboards were as blaaack as coal!"

Maman had trembled. "*Il y a de la glace dans les veines de celle-là.*"

Jackytar

"Why didn't you say something," I childishly questioned.

She'd looked disconsolately at the organ, "Alexandre, *on répond aux imbéciles par le silence!*"

I hugged her, sat in the pew and quietly watched her practise. That day, her feet played the pedals and her hands flew over the keyboards like magic. The music reverberated in my chest, filling my soul, I liked to imagine, with…now her brief periods of magic at the organ were forever gone. I was apprehensive about seeing her again. Nothing lasts forever.

We drove to the hospital in solemn silence. It was pouring. I struggled through the metal doors of St. Matthew's Hospital after Bruce and Dad, barring the door behind me against the violent windy rainstorm that threatened to knock us down. I stomped the rain off my boots as best I could but the mat was wet as dung; so as I walked, my boots squished embarrassingly. The last time I'd spoken with Maman was two and a half weeks ago. I'd just returned home from an early movie with Keith. She'd left me a message on the answering machine. Since this was uncommon, I'd called her back immediately even though it was late and we'd chatted for a few minutes. She'd sounded normal – somewhat morose and monotone, perhaps a bit more anxious than usual, but relatively normal for her. Little did I know even then she'd been sick. I stuffed my leather gloves in my pocket and took down my hood. My hair felt damp and tangled. I didn't care. There were more pressing matters at hand.

"Dad, you lead the way. I don't know where to turn," I said. The grey-haired man at the reception desk smiled as we entered.

"Some awful we'tter! Who you here to see, sir?"

"Sure is. Oi'm Julian Murphy. Here to see m'poor wife, France Murphy."

The man nodded understandingly. "You knows the way?"

"He-yeah," said Dad with a sharp intake of air, making that throaty sound that exists in the Atlantic Provinces but no where else to my knowledge and is impossible to transcribe. "T'ank you."

I undid my raglan as we made our glum procession down the unfamiliar halls. Our footsteps echoed on the dull tiled floor, a foreboding tam-tam to the tableau of sickness and death awaiting us. The tiles were brownish with age and smelled faintly of bleach. This was the palliative care ward, I realized. We passed a parade of agonised family members and friends of other patients. Some patients were old, some younger, I noticed, as many doors were wide open, lending a sense of illicit openness to what was an intimate rite of passage into death. I felt like a Peeping Tom. Most patients were bedridden, except for two. An elderly man walked stubbornly down the corridor, his lower lip curled with determination, clanking his walker on the floor. An attractive young woman in her late twenties pushed a withered man in a wheelchair, talking softly. His head lolled to one side. She was either his daughter or his wife. His grey-flecked hair was lifeless and the skin of his face was tight to his skull yet unlined. His eyes were innocent like an infant's and I doubted he understood a soothing word she was saying.

Where were the nurses, nursing aides, janitors, and doctors? The ward appeared deserted, although a steaming cup of coffee on the nurses' counter indicated some

Jackytar

presence. We turned left and confronted a door of thick, double-plated glass. A petite old woman wearing a stained nightgown leaned on an aluminium cane. Her watery eyes locked on mine. She motioned for me to move closer with her claw-like hand.

Her whisper was strangled and piteous. "Will you pleeease let me ooout? I waaants to go ooome!" Her bottom lip trembled. She reached out to touch me but the glass obstructed her. I recoiled as if she were the Grim Reaper.

I looked around in vain for a nurse.

"C'mon," said Bruce, "they got old people here wid Ole Timer's. She's awright, b'y."

"Sorry, ma'am," I muttered to the old lady. Embarrassed and a bit panicky, I left her standing there, staring after us. We continued further down the hallway, past an open linen closet and halted in the doorway of room 123.

"Be prepared," said Dad. Bruce nodded.

This was a relatively large room with two armchairs, an empty closet to the left, a bathroom to the right, and a large curtained window on the far side. A fan circulated a breeze. There was another bed opposite hers, curtained off. I heard murmurs and the sounds of water swishing. A nurse was giving a patient a sponge bath. I looked for Maman. The tiny figure in the centre of the bed was a stranger to me. Her mouth hung open and her greying brown hair was dry, cotton-like and uncombed. She had always taken care of her hair, even if she kept it shortly cropped. Sheets enshrouded her up to the neck. Her lower left leg and foot lay forlornly outside.

I rushed to the bed and clutched the metal bed rails.

This isn't Maman, I thought, staring at the face of the woman on the bed. My heart palpitated as I brought my hand to hers. Whatever disease was ravaging her brain was causing her temperature to be elevated. The angles of her face were sharp, haggard now. And I recognized her hands – the long slim fingers that played the piano and especially the organ with such sureness and feeling. The only thing that had ever really enthused her was her music.

"How could she have deteriorated so quickly?" I asked.

"Twas very quick. A month or so ago she seemed fine. Tumours can be like that," said Dad. "Fine one day and yer on yer way out the next."

I hung my dripping raglan in the closet. Everything was either plastic or chrome here. Bruce and Dad stood over her bed and I sat on a chair by her side.

"She's some bad," said Bruce.

I covered her naked foot and calf with the end of the bed sheet. The nurse from across the room opened the curtains. The inhabitant of the bed was a hairless woman of about seventy years. The patient managed a weak smile. We greeted her and she closed her eyes. After formalities, the nurse spoke.

"Yer mother's specialist will come in shortly."

After about forty minutes, the doctor showed up. He was a small man with a wizened face. He led us out to a little lounge, decorated with plastic-looking yellow armchairs. I sat on the matching couch. Springs dug into my rear end.

"We have the results of her new tests and it's confirmed," said Dr. Dobbin compassionately. "The tumour is in a part of her brain that makes it impossible to

*J*acky*tar*

operate without causing massive damage to brain tissue and paralysing her." He gestured with his hands. His nails were immaculate. "The tumour is like an octopus on back of her head, sending tentacles into her brain that are impossible to remove. It's affecting her central nervous system and brain centre. Minute aneurysms are erupting in her head.

"You can expect her to wake periodically but she's probably not going to make much sense. She might not even recognize you. She's not eating so we've got her hooked up to intravenous." He paused and looked at each of us in turn, finally settling on Dad. "She might last a few days more and she could be gone anytime. Our duty now is to try and keep her comfortable. I'm sorry. I wish there was more we could do."

"Are you sure you can't operate. What if we flew her to Halifax or Toronto?" I asked.

"I checked with colleagues and it's unanimous. No surgeon will operate on this particular form of tumour. I'm very sorry."

Bruce didn't say much but I knew by the way he averted his eyes that he was suffering. Bruce, the brother I'd always thought never had a heart. Dad, on the other hand, swallowed hard and looked at me.

"That's all she wrote, b'y. That's all she wrote."

I rested my hand on his shoulder.

s e v e n

■

Waiting for someone to die is a vigil suffused with loneliness, regret and a sense of futility. Dad shifted constantly in his chair, frequently getting up to stretch his legs. But he didn't dare go far. His arthritis had worsened over the years, just like Poppy Murphy, and I knew this damp, cold weather must be hell for him. He gently bathed Maman's face with a damp washcloth and then stroked her still lovely hands. His face bore an august air. His eyes were watery and nostalgic. He accepted the inevitable and I realized that I must, too.

I sat in the armchair by her side, hoping she'd wake up if only for a minute, a few seconds. And I watched his ministrations in wonder. I recognized, with shock, that he might actually love her. Given their tumultuous history, the thought had never occurred to me before. In fact, I guiltily thought that she hadn't deserved many of the countless niceties he'd bestowed on her over the years, from doing most of the yard and housework, to preparing meals and tending to our guests. Even when he brought her some of her beloved and expensive music books from St. John's, he was lucky if she'd respond with a terse *merci*.

Now that she was dying, I had erroneously assumed that he wouldn't miss her one iota. That he might even be filled with relief. I'd always suspected that they hated each other, that they were in what talk show hosts called an unhealthy co-dependant relationship. Perhaps I'd been wrong. Or was my father a sucker? Even though immobile, unable to torture him with her moodiness and disapproval, was she manipulating him into being her personal nurse right up until her last gasp?

I was pondering the bizarre dynamics of their relationship when Evelyn suggested that she and Bruce go for coffee and a muffin in the hospital cafeteria.

"No maid, I idden particularly hungry or thirsty," Bruce protested.

"But it's half past three. My blood sugar level is getting low. It'll do you good, too, to move your limbs, honey," she coaxed, "and I'd like your company."

He reluctantly marched off with her, his forehead wrinkled. She wanted Dad and me to be alone for a few minutes with Maman. How sensitive of her, I thought.

"How ya doing?" I asked, as soon as my brother and sister-in-law had departed.

"Oh, awright, I spose. I never thought she'd be gone before me. Oi'm gettin older, too, right. And m'breathin problems are worse. I uses the puffer more and more. Other than that, I do feel hale and hearty enough, I spose."

As if to illustrate his point, or perhaps subconsciously, he took the puffer from his the inside pocket of his jacket, shook it and inhaled deeply twice. So much of what we do is subconscious.

"Ya never know, eh?" I said. "Dad, when did ya notice she was getting sick?"

He looked at me with wide blue eyes. I observed something of an innocence there I'd rarely detected before, or perhaps a vulnerability, and it startled me. "Well, to be honest, like they says, hindsight is twenty-twenty. I guess I really started noticin changes about a month ago. But they were small.

"Ya knows yer mudder! We never did talk much. She kept pretty much to herself, right. I mean, a few year ago, she hooked ap wid Rev. Byrne. That done her a world a good. She started playin the argan at the church after Aunt Flo gave it ap. But as for her attitude at home, not a whole lot a difference! At least she was gettin out. Always doing somethin down at St. Stephen's Church. People raved about her, ya know? Twas a major improvement."

"Surprising, eh?" I said. "She was never very sociable."

"Ya don't need to tell me. Christ, most of the time I knowed her, she'd rather be holed ap alone wid no one to bother her. That being said, I didn't begrudge her this change, even if she was still a hard case at home." He leaned towards me and lowered his voice. "Then about a month ago, she started actin strange, see? She was makin mistakes playin her hymns. Cursin in French. And yer mudder never did that before. Then I started to notice that she wasn't playin the argan as often. One day, twas real quiet, right, I crept ap to her door. So I goes to the door, knocks softly, but she wouldn't answer. So I opens the door a crack, see, and peeks inside. There she was, sound asleep on the armchair, snorin like a lumberjack. I closes the door and goes about m'business and checks back suppertime to

Jackytar

wake her. She started takin naps all the time."

He rubbed his temple. "Then it got worse. She used to go downstairs in the marnin and instead a goin to her music room, she'd sit at the kitchen table for the longest time, drinkin tay or just starin out the window."

"Was there anything else?" I asked.

"He-yeah, her appetite got worse and she was losin weight. Rev. Byrne rung me up one day. She was actin weird at church, too. Missin practises. Making mistakes when she played. So I tried to talk to her again. Begged her to see the doctor, but she refused. Said she was right as rain and warned me to leave her alone, in that tone of hers that could curdle –"

"So did you contact a doctor yourself?"

He motioned for me to stop. "Hold on to yer jigger! Oi'm gettin to that."

I noticed the thick copper bracelet around his wrist to ward off the arthritis. I couldn't recall if this was a placebo. But if it worked.

"Then her speech got funny. She stuttered and forgot words. Sometimes she used the wrong word altogether! So I called the clinic despite her wishes and the doctor made a house call. France was roary eyed mad. He said he wasn't sure and didn't want to speculate, so he ordered some tests. We managed to git her over to the clinic."

"That couldn't have been easy," I said.

"By that time, she was worried herself. I tried to keep an eye on her. A few days went by and the doctor called us back. He set up an appointment for her wid a neurologist in St. John's for the very next day! So we packed her up and drove her in. And hh…here we are today."

"Are you okay, Dad?"

"Oi'm grand. Just a bit thirsty, s'all." He poured himself a glass of cold water in a paper cup from the washroom and chugged it down. He resumed stroking Maman's hand and arm. "Frenchie, m'ducky, we've been through somethin, haven't we?"

We sat in silence for some time.

Evelyn and Bruce appeared at the door.

"Hey, we brought you back some snacks," she said.

"Thanks." I took a granola bar and coffee from her. Bruce handed Dad a coffee. He declined the food.

"I spose she'll be free from it all soon enough," said Dad, blinking away tears. "He-yeah, soon enough Frenchie…"

Jackytar

e i g h t

■

That evening, at her bedside vigil, I plugged in my laptop and began writing. The cheapest therapy available. The other patient in the room was also asleep. After all day, I'd convinced Dad, Bruce and Evelyn to take a break and go for a quick bite in the cafeteria. I swore I'd summon them if Maman's condition changed. Dr. Dobbin intended to cut back on the morphine in her drip so she might be more awake and coherent later on. Dad seemed sentimental and conflicted, a tortured soul. The depth of his feelings for Maman surprised me.

When I was a boy, he'd sometimes have his army buddies over. They'd drink Newfie Screech and homemade blueberry wine and toast the queen and country – Newfoundland and Great Britain, not Canada. They'd play cards, usually One Hundred and Twenty. Loud guffaws would echo through Torbay House, along with the pounding of fists on the kitchen table and then, once they'd played for hours, the yarning would begin. Oh how they yarned! Dad always reigned supreme. He'd tie in a healthy dose of humour but often skate around to a serious moral. How I loved his yarns! I'd listen at the top of the stairs hidden from view until someone noticed me and yelled for me to get to bed.

He was usually the one to tuck me in. Tall as a giant but gentle as a lamb. And he would lull me to sleep with a yarn. I thought of my favourite yarn.

"The Big Spud"

Little Eddy lived in an old two-story bungalow in Bond Cove with his mother and three brothers. His father had died in the Great War. The boys all went to school during the day but they all had chores. His older brothers hunted rabbits, grouse, partridge, and moose. They also cut logs in the woods. Little Eddy's brothers then sawed the logs into stove-sized junks and clove them into splits. Every day, Little Eddy lugged yaffels of wood into the porch and stowed them away in the wood box. They used a wood stove to cook with and heat the house. His mother baked many loaves of bread, lining the kitchen counter like baby quintuplets in swaddling clothes as they cooled. She pre-pared huge boilers of hearty soup and stew. They kept chickens. They also had a vegetable garden behind the house that provided lettuce, cabbage, turnips, beets, carrots, and potatoes.

Planting potatoes the first week of June and taking care of the potato patch was another one

Jackytar

of Little Eddy's chores. He and his brothers cut potatoes into two pieces with at least two eyes on each piece, which they then called seed potatoes. They had already made drills and spread the manure. This day, the boys ran up the hill behind their house to the garden. The boys added the seed one-foot apart and then filled in the drills. Little Eddy was excellent at planting potatoes, better than any of his brothers were. He soon had three drills done while most of his brothers had only two. Within a couple of hours, the job was done.

Everyone waited until Herman, the eldest, spoke. "A bit of rain and lots of sunshine, and we should have a good crop this year."

Everyone agreed that Little Eddy would once again be in charge of the potatoes, making sure that dogs, goats and sheep didn't get in and tear it up. Then the strangest weather came to Bond Cove. It rained for two weeks, followed by two weeks of pure sunshine, and then more heavy rain!

The day soon came when Little Eddy was asked to go trench the potatoes, to add more ground to the growing stalks. He went to the shed and got a pointed shovel. He walked up the grassy hill and began to examine a potato stalk.

Strange? The stalks seemed…connected to each other!

He dug his hands into the dirt.

DOUGLAS GOSSE

"Wow!" he cried. "What in the world's goin on?"

He began clearing more soil off the potato with his bare hands. The more he cleared, the larger the potato looked.

Little Eddy bolted to his feet and ran back to the house, his eyes wide and blinking like Bullet in a snow starm. "Everyone, come quick to the potato patch!"

"Wow!" they all said, one by one, as they neared the potato patch. Herman, the last to arrive, grabbed a shovel from the shed and shovelled away with all his might.

A hush fell over the children. Little Eddy spoke softly. "That's the biggest spud I ever did see!"

Weeks sped by and the potato grew steadily bigger, until it was larger than their neat bungalow. They tried some. The potato tasted normal, boiled or mashed, despite its unusual size. People came from all over the Avalon Peninsula to view the monster potato, heralded in the newspaper as "the Big Spud." They often took Little Eddy's picture beside it.

The Big Spud became so ungainly that Little Eddy's mother told the people of Bond Cove they could take all the potato they wanted. Little Eddy cheerfully filled their buckets with potato. They nicknamed him "the Spud Boy."

Then one day, Little Eddy's mother called him into the parlour. "Oi'm afraid the Big Spud may

Jackytar

tumble down the hill," she said. "It has to go. Tomorrow marnin."

Little Eddy was sad, but he understood.

The next day, the family rose at the crack of dawn. After a breakfast of molasses bread and tay, they went outdoors to begin Operation Big Spud. As the minutes passed, people from all over arrived with picks and shovels.

Dirt flew through the air as people worked side by side around the Big Spud. Little Eddy pitched in. The Big Spud wouldn't move. Adults whispered to Little Eddy's mother and then spoke to the tractor operators.

The tractors roared to life, attacking the Big Spud from the sides. Little Eddy felt a tremor beneath his feet. People gasped and moved back.

"It's like an iceberg!" screamed Little Eddy over the noise of the crowd. "Git back! Quick!"

The Big Spud began to roll. People scattered like sawdust in the wind, parents gathered their young ones in their arms and dashed for safety.

The Big Spud tottered on the top of the hill. Little Eddy held his breath.

The Big Spud then rolled and bounced down the hill, squatting a wheelbarrow in its path, moving faster and faster.

"Ah!" cried the crowd, as it headed out of harm's way. "Oh!" as its direction changed.

Boom!

DOUGLAS GOSSE

It smashed into the bungalow, sending wood splintering far into the surrounding countryside. The Big Spud came to a halt. Simultaneously, the crowd edged forward. No one was hurt. They stood a cautious distance from the Big Spud.

Flames flickered from beneath the Big Spud, sitting majestically among the ruins of their bungalow. The wood stove had been lit and caught the house on fire.

Bond Covians crowded around the family.

"Don't you worry," assured Mr. and Mrs. Cardwell, owners of a local saw mill. "We'll git ye a new house, better than the last one."

"Here! Here!" agreed a number of people. "We'll build it fore ya knows it!"

"We'll git ye all new clothes, m'dears," said someone from the church, "and pots and pans and everything else ye needs!"

Little Eddy gazed at the fire. The aroma of baked potato filled the air.

"I know!" he said excitedly. "Let's have a baked potato roast!"

His mother thought about it and laughed despite the tears. "I think that's a marvellous idea!"

They all watched until the fire had burned down. Then Little Eddy and his brothers handed out portions, roasted to perfection.

Within two weeks, the family had a new, neat bungalow, even nicer than their old one.

Jackytar

The Big Spud became a local legend and Little Eddy was forever known as the Spud Boy, a title he bore with pride.

The End

I wrote furiously on my computer. Happy memories as Dad tucked me into bed and told me that yarn for the hundredth time. I never tired of it. I wondered if the story incarnated aspects of his own childhood – the heroic father and his legacy, the noble mother, his loneliness at being an only child? Could Dad have felt he was like Little Eddy as a boy, having to prove his manhood, this big strapping Viking of a man, my father?

Funny how no two stories are ever alike, even when the same story is told over and over again. Fiction fluctuates. Fact does too.

Ah, the power of yarning!

Maybe as he'd aged, Dad had grown increasingly sentimental about his marriage and his new yarns reflected this process. I contemplated Maman's wasted body and was overcome with pity. Like Dad, I stroked one of her hands, then the other. No reaction but I detected life in them. Lingering. Refusing to let go. But Maman would play the organ no more, I knew in my heart.

How she used to hate that name – Frenchie.

"Yer fadder, he call me Frenchie, but anyone else!" she told me once, waving her fist in the air.

She had shown sparks of zeal. Sparks for more than just organ music, I realized. Memories of her mental illness had made me almost forget. Once, I'd just come home from school and she'd noticed that I was upset. She coaxed me into telling her about the bullying, being called Jackytar.

But I edited the part about being called a fag.

"*Ah mon fils*, they ear a French accent and they think you'm a bloody uneducated Jackytar from the Port-au-Port. You don't even ave an accent in English or in French. Yer lucky. Yer bilingual. You can go anywhere. I tell ya one thing – we have a proud history. *Savoir d'où on vient, c'est aussi savoir où on va! C'est ce qu'on dit chez nous. N'oublie pas, hein?*"

And I hadn't forgotten.

I looked at her anew, lying at death's door. I longed to hear her stories – her yarns, but that was no longer possible.

I filled a paper cup with cold water and tilted her head gently backwards to help her drink. It was a reflex, the drinking. Like so much in life.

Déclic!

Suddenly, I felt ashamed. Like when I walked by those homeless Natives holding out cups in Toronto. Ashamed of looking in the mirror and refusing to see anyone but a white man. Ashamed of ignoring that crucial part of my maternal heritage. Maman was mixed, so therefore I was, too. Maybe Bruce chose to ignore that side of himself, but I vowed to no more. In homage to her.

In homage to our ancestors.

Guilt no more. A new beginning.

As me.

"*Je te le promets*, Maman! I promise!"

I didn't get to speak anymore with Dad alone that day but I knew I needed to break the patterns of silence in my life. It was too late for Maman to reconcile with Dad, Bruce, or myself, but it wasn't too late for the rest of

Jackytar

us. I craved active acceptance, not benign tolerance. A confrontation was imminent and I hoped we could have one built of love.

Déclic!

I thought of my church in Toronto, of the newcomers, gay and straight, who wept upon experiencing a place of joy and acceptance on their first visit. So different from most of the churches I'd experienced. And I thought of our pastor, Rev. Dr. Brent Hawkes, his exegetic preaching and earnest tone, the intermittent jokes, the modern yarns tied in with biblical scripture, and I recalled this yarn he told:

> Two brothers who were farmers lived on adjoining properties. For many years they shared equipment and work. Eventually, they had a falling out and stopped talking to one another. A traveller came by one day and asked Pete, one of the brothers, "Do ya have any work for me?"
>
> Pete showed him the creek separating his farm from his brother's property and said, "Yes, I want you to build a fence there."
>
> Pete gave him the tools and supplies and went into town for a while. When he returned, he was shocked to discover that instead of a fence, the brother had built a bridge and his brother was walking across it. Before he had time to protest, his brother embraced him and said, "After all I've done, I can't believe you built a bridge!"

The brothers reconciled and the carpenter started walking away.

"Wait," said Pete, "I have more work for you."

The carpenter turned and replied, "No, I must go. I have more bridges to build."

Building bridges with my father and brother was a goal I wanted to accomplish. Beginning with forgiveness. They didn't realize how much they hurt me.

Was it even possible?

We left the hospital late. The nurse told us to go home and get some sleep and swore to call us if her condition worsened. Dad kissed Maman on the cheek before he left.

Jackytar

n i n e

■

Our Father who art in heaven,
Hallowed be thy name;
Thy...dominion come;
Thy will be done on earth as it is in heaven.
Give us this day our daily bread;
And forgive us our debts,
As we forgive our debtors.
And lead us not into temptation, but deliver us from evil;
For thine is...dominion.
And the power and the glory,
For ever. Amen.

t e n

■

A knock at the door. Excitement!

"Maman, *c'est qui ça?*"

"*Chais pas. J'vas aller voir!*"

Bruce and I hid behind her as she opened the door. She smelled good. Her gold locket was her only jewellery. They clamoured in.

Three mummers!

The biggest one wore a sou'wester on his head, a ratty fur coat slung over his shoulders and baggy old woman's drawers on the outside of his overalls. The middle one had her clothes on backwards and carried a birch switch. Or was it a man? The little one wore oil skins on top and a plaid skirt over long underwear below. Their faces were covered in bright scarves and sunglasses.

"Merry Christmas! C'mon in!" said Maman, laughing. "My, don't ye all look some foolish! *Franchement!*" She took the birch switch the middle one carried. "You leave that right ere in the porch!" she ordered. "Ye won't be chasin no one in this ouse tonight!"

She led them into the kitchen where a cosy fire blazed in the woodstove.

"Youse must be sweatin," she said. They shook their head. "I spose I gotta fed ye and give ye a drink, right? *Du whiskey?*"

They nodded vigorously. The little one made out like he was dying of thirst. Maman laid a platter of cookies on the table. Then she retrieved the whiskey bottle from under the sink and poured drinks. Bruce and I sat at the kitchen table, spellbound.

They gestured a lot. The little one put a cassette in the tape recorder. An Irish jig came on. Maman handed them their whiskey, smiling all the while.

The mummers downed their drinks and started to dance. A big balled up hockey sock fell out of the middle mummer's sweater and the mummer grabbed it off the floor and stuffed it back in. Everyone laughed.

Bruce clapped his hands and tried to sing along but he didn't know the words. I hummed and stole a cookie.

The little one grunted and motioned for Maman to pour more drinks. She turned to the counter and took the stopper off the whiskey bottle.

"One more! But ye gotta sing us a song when yer ready!"

The middle one and the little one started to sing. The bigger mummer grabbed Bruce and started to dance with him. He held him high in the air above his head, spinning around. Maman turned around as he pretended to throw him out the window. Bruce squealed in delight.

Maman dropped the bottle and it crashed to the floor. "*Donne-moi mon bébé*! My baby!" she screamed.

The little one turned the music off. The middle one froze. The big one swore and tore his scarf and glasses off.

Bruce and I started to cry.

"Jaysus, France! Ya just about gave me a heart attack! What's the hell's wrong?"

She snatched Bruce from his arms.

It was Dad.

Jackytar

e l e v e n

■

Mon*day*

We all rose early in order to get over to the hospital as soon as possible. That morning at breakfast, Dad and I found ourselves alone once again. Bruce and Evelyn were getting ready. It was supposed to rain and black clouds loomed overhead. I remembered the dream from last night and my gut ached. I poured us both steaming cups of coffee, determined to embark on my new motto: break those silences!

"She hardly budged all evenin, eh?" said Dad.

"Well, hopefully this morning she'll be more alert. I called the hospital first thing. Dr. Dobbin cut down on the morphine." We both chose cold cereal with skim milk and blueberries. "Dad, do you remember the time the mummers came into our house. You were one of them?"

"Jaysus, Alex. I thought someone was kilt! You remembers that. Ya weren't very ole."

"I dreamt about it last night."

"Christ, we had our trials wid er, didn't we?"

He cleared the newspaper off the table and sat down to eat.

"By the way, Dad, you said something earlier that puzzles me. As long as I can remember, for want of a better term, Maman was emotionally fragile. You said she hadn't always been that way. That you'd known her in better times. Do you mind telling me more about that?"

He cleared his throat. "Nope, not a'tol. I wants to git it all off me chest. Been too long keepin it bottled up inside. We should a let everything out in the open years ago."

I wasn't entirely surprised at his openness. He'd always been one for spinning yarns, entertaining guests and telling us bedtime stories. Now that Maman lay dying, he coped by sharing their past together, as if the act of yarning could lessen his suffering or...guilt?

"Well, in that case, go ahead. Just don't feel you have to."

He finished up his cereal and held the coffee cup in his hands. He looked past me into the distance where the Atlantic Ocean toyed with people's lives.

"Oi'm gonna go back a few years now and start from the beginnin. Yer mudder's lyin on her deathbed, so tidden like Oi'm talkin behind her back. I wouldn't do that. And I spose none if it matters much anymore. I guess, in a way, I wants some resolution. Resolution she could never give me, so this is m'way a goin about it."

I nodded. He was in a yarning mood. His eyes squinted and his voice deepened and grew more intimate. This was a time for listening, for me to be silent.

"Yer mudder and I met when I was in the army, finishin up a stint as staff sergeant down on the base in Quidi Vidi. We had a little officer's club we'd be invited to on special occasions and this was the closin ceremony for a bunch of us who'd served our time and were gettin out. Movin on to bigger and better things, we thought.

Jackytar

"The Officer's Club was located in a tidy little house on Gerard Street, which in those days was a fine neighbourhood, and is again from what I understands. Yer mudder worked for a rich family. The man was a skipper on the boats and his wife was from a very old St. John's family. She had it good there. Three square meals a day. A decent salary in those days, more than what she'd had back home on the Port-au-Port Peninsula among the Jackytars."

He said "Jackytars" as if it was a bad word and I winced.

"Jaysus! We went up there once after youse was born. France wanted to surprise her mudder. They'd lost touch after she moved to town. They had no phone, so we drove up. We left youse in Bond Cove wid Mom and Dad. I'll never forget it. They were livin like a hundred year ago. Yer mudder's people never even had electricity and this was only…thirty odd year ago! They still cut wood for the woodstove. That was one thing the b'ys did. I'll give em credit for that. Their house was little more than a shack. The missus kept it clean but the furniture was some shabby. Ya'd think her brudders would a painted the house, eh? A bit a paint don't cost much, especially back then. Indians they were. Well, part Micmac, anyway. He-yeah, and French, too.

"The ole woman barely spoke a word a English. She was dark like yer mudder but her brudders, they was even more Indian lookin than she, as if they never had a bit a French or English in em! I wouldn't doubt but that they all had different fadders. The skipper had passed away when France was a little girl, from too much drink. She never spoke much about that. She couldn't even remember un.

"Alex, they never even had a bathtub…which in all fairness wasn't too uncommon in rural Newfoundland in those days. The only tilet they had was an ole outhouse out back and you could smell it from a mile away! Jaysus! Some shockin twas. A bit a lime wouldn't a gone astray!

"And the missus, apparently she'd been pretty good lookin in her day, but now she was fat. Not just plump or matronly, but rolls a fat on her neck, on her droopy arms, and her gut was like she was nine months pregnant. She had her hair all done up in a braid, just like the squaw and ciled around her head. The steps to the porch was half rotten. You'd hardly believe it. And those big men, her sons, loungin around. One of them was lyin on the woodbox, a pillow under his head, when we went in. Didn't even bot'er to git ap. Claude, twas. I didn't like un from the start. The other two was awright I spose. Got up and shook m'hand like ya would."

I used to romanticize a large woman who spoke French. A noble woman who had suffered. A small house and the sweet smell of wood burning as she cooked over a woodstove, turning and chatting with Maman. I imagined uncles coming in and patting me on the head, speaking quickly in the language we all understood.

"Well, we landed there and tookt off our coats. The missus smiled at me and spoke some pidgin English. 'Me *nom* iz Bernadette.' I sat down at the kitchen table and was makin conversation wid her two younger brudders. Their English weren't too bad. They were polite enough. When France told them we was married, they slapped me on the back. All cept Claude. He never budged from the woodbox. I went out to the truck and brought in a box a groceries for em. Some tinned food from St. John's. Some nice fabric and knittin wool for yer grandmudder.

"Then yer mudder went in the living room wid your

Jackytar

grandmudder. Initially yer grandmudder seemed pleased. The brudders offered me some whiskey but I knowed yer mudder wouldn't be pleased if I drank, so I didn't take none. They were yappin away in French for a while, France and she. France was showin the missus our family photo album and suddenly t'all grew quiet. So quiet you could hear a pin drop, my son! I went out and asked yer mudder what was wrong."

He paused and shook his head, staring at me intently.

"Go on," I urged.

"Well, she ignored me. Then they started gettin louder and louder. The missus was agitated. Came out of the living room into the kitchen, pointin and wavin her finger around. None of us seemed to have a clue what was goin on. 'What's wrong, France?' I said.

"She wouldn't answer. I tried to git her brudders to talk wid me but they clammed ap. Then, bozo, the one that had been lyin on the woodbox, got into it. He was a big son of a bitch, too. He grabbed me by the shirt and said somethin in French. I tried to back off and the other brudder, Thomas, got in the middle, thank God, cause I swears to ya, one of us would a been kilt.

"By this time, yer mudder was frantic. The missus was wailin like a banshee and the other son, Jean-Marc, he was tryin to calm em both down. Then France grabbed me by the coat and fairly dragged me out the door.

"'Wait, France,' I says and before she can stop me, I races back into the house. I comes back out a few minutes later wid her pump argan. Her brudders, Thomas and Jean-Marc, helped me lug it into the back a the truck. They seemed as mystified as me. We roped it down and finally we tookt off, the two brudders by the shoulder a the road as we drove off! We stopped in a gravel pit outside a town. Tookt me an hour to git any sense out of her. She was holdin her head in her hands and bawlin. Twas right awful!"

"What'd happened?" I asked.

At that moment, Bruce stormed in. "I just got a call from the hospital on my cell phone. She had a seizure. Let's go!"

t w e l v e

■

I missed my church in Toronto. I missed the joy, passion and celebration of the choir, their faces shining like angels. I missed the lesbian, gay, bisexual, transsexual, transgendered and straight folks who surrounded me and openly wiped tears from their eyes and sang loudly and prayed intently and raised their arms in the air, something I was always too uneasy to do. I missed hearing the parts of the Eucharist that the pastor and deacon sang in touchingly amateurish voices that we responded to in unison. I missed the sincerity of my pastor, Rev. Dr. Brent Hawkes, and his sermons that always made me reflect on the past week and confront the coming week with a little more compassion and love in my heart.

What was it Rev. Dr. Brent Hawkes had said last Sunday, as if he were speaking solely to me?

"We're constantly reaching out to others. People hurt each other, sometimes particularly parents and their children. What can we do when the disappointments, resentments and hurt are in our most important relationship? Row after row, we nurture our resentments and self-pity. There is always the threat that we will allow our fears, shame and resentment of the past to not allow us to be happy in the present."

I thought of that sermon as we hurried into the hospital towards her room, expecting the worse, only to find her in the same catatonic state as yesterday. We summoned Dr. Dobbin.

"She had a bad bout for a few minutes. Another seizure like that and she won't last long. Another day. Maybe two," he warned. "She may wake up at any time but expect delirium."

We didn't have relatives in town that we knew of and Maman wouldn't have wanted a crowd visiting anyhow, private as she was. I was already referring to her in the past tense, someone who was, yet who soon would be no more. Then again, how much, really, had she ever been with any of us, even while alive and conscious?

My mind and heart were preparing to accept her death and, hopefully, her passage into a better place. Evelyn took out a book. We had barely settled in when Bruce spoke up.

"Look, she's stirring!"

Sure enough, her legs and arms twitched. Her brown eyes flew open.

"Help her to sit ap. Quick!" said Dad.

While Bruce operated the mechanized bed, Dad and I took her by the arms and pulled her light body higher on the pillows. Her arms felt like they were made of feather. No bone or meat left on her.

"Maman, can you hear me? It's Alex. *C'est moi, ton fils.*"

Her rheumy eyes showed a glimmer of recognition. She looked back and forth and I wasn't sure if she could

Jackytar

tell who was who. Evelyn remained in the armchair, sensitively leaving room for blood relatives.

"France, can ya hear me? How are ya, m'love?"

Dad spoke gently. He laid his right hand on her shoulder and the other on her thigh. She looked at him.

"Thirsty," she said, hardly audible.

Evelyn jumped up and returned a few seconds later with a paper cup of water. Dad held it to her lips. Some water dribbled over, which I wiped with a tissue. She began speaking but it was a tirade of words, French and English, that made little sense. We were bewildered. Although the doctor had informed us it might be sudden like this, the reality of it was surreal. Bits of memories from yesteryears that fell into unintelligible whispers.

"And tell them that Claude and Thomas…*devraient aller chercher leur kit…aller sur la mer*…tis cold ya knows. That tastes some good…*la morue…Maman a toujours dit que j'etais la plus forte*…git away…the chandelier's like the light of the ange…*le pauvre petit ange*…me hands *tellement sales*…they always said that that I knows what they're like…don't listen…*ne les écoute pas la!…chus fatiguée*."

She was agitated. She shook her arm and her lips quivered like that of a woman thirty years her senior.

"Maman, we're all here – Bruce, Dad and me and Evelyn, your daughter-in-law. We're here. Try to relax. Well take care of you."

"*Dis-moi*…youse is all gonna go to the church…tis so beautiful…that minister and Mr. and Mrs. Powers…I told them they was eating the Communion bread…*hostie*…and the Lard spoke and told them…but the baby was so young…weak and frail…*frêle comme une petite colombe blanche allant vers dieu*…"

She began weeping, huge tears coursing down her sallow cheeks, but she was too weak to rise. Evelyn passed Dad another tissue. He wiped her tears away.

"*L'église est notre parent…faut y faire confiance…*love and the argan music in the church…gotta go to play the argan…practise for the Christmas show…*je dois jouer pour les enfants pour pardonner…Saint Seigneur, pardonne-moi!*"

"Alex, what's she sayin, m'son. I can't pick hide nor hair out of it."

Bruce looked sheepish, like a young boy unsure of his role in all of this. Selfishly, I was glad to be called upon because of my fluency in French, fluency Bruce had never gained.

"I really don't know," I said. "Sorry, but I can't pick much sense out of it either. Half the words I can't even hear. All I can pick out is something about a baby and children and church."

Wired and weak as she was, she tired herself out quickly. A nurse came by and after consultation with Dr. Dobbin, gave her a sedative. She drifted into a deep sleep, her breathing heavy and her forehead sweaty. The nurse closed the curtains and informed us she was about to give her a sponge bath.

"Now go on to the cafeteria. We got everything here under control. Don't worry."

She repeated her assurances to Dad who was reluctant to leave. "Look, she's out now for another hour at least. Maybe more. Don't worry. But expect her to be incoherent again when she comes to. Nothing we can do about that."

Jackytar

"Can you call me on my cell phone if anything happens?" said Bruce.

"We really want to know. We want to be by her side," I added.

The nurse looked me over. "I promise." Bruce handed her his number. "Look, I'll wash her up. That'll soothe her. We could use a bit of privacy. Her vital signs are weak but she's not going anywhere quite yet!" She looked at me. "You're not from here, are ya?"

"Born and bred but living in Toronto now," I said.

"Whatcha doin up there?"

"I'm an instructor at Ontario College."

"Whattaya teach?"

"French and English," I replied. "Second language and multiculturalism."

"I guess you need that up there, eh? I lived there in Brampton for six years with my husband and two kids. We called it Bramladesh. Then we came home out of it. Back to the Rock."

She laughed, this straight-forward talking, solidly-built woman in her fifties. Her hair was a shellacked corn yellow with grey-brown roots. A gold cross hung around her neck. She looked like she could handle just about anything that came her way. I was hungry and thought we all could use a break, particularly Dad, with his ashen face and nervous hands. Bruce still had that lingering little boy look, as if he didn't quite know where to put his arms and legs. The nurse peered into my face.

"Sometimes I was the only white woman in the subway car in the morning. Imagine! What's it like up there these days?"

t h i r t e e n

■

"So, you miss me, huh?"

I held the phone tentatively pressed against my ear, this machine through which I heard a distant voice.

I said: Yeah, of course I do.

He said: How's your mother?

I paused. Which words could express what I was going through? Did he even care, this partner of mine?

I said: She's not going to last. We're waiting.

There was a pause. Could he even find false words of sympathy or comfort anymore?

I thought not. He was too far gone. His mind changed. His body taken over. I wondered if he would ever return to me.

Instead I asked: How have you been doing?

He said: Whattaya mean?

I exhaled and said: Well, you know what I mean.

He launched into a harangue: I'm fine. Why do you keep harping on this? I'm a big boy. I can take care of myself. I don't need anybody's help. Been working long hours on Bay Street so both of us can live well and travel and buy nice clothes and things for the condo, and retire with a cottage up North.

He has a plan. Nothing will get in the way of the plan. His plan.

I held the phone away from my ear.

His voice turned gentler. He reassured me that he missed me. Loves me. Can't live without me. Will always be there.

I said: G'night. Lots of love. Be careful.

Déclic!

Stuck. I was stuck as sure as it was raining this evening. As sure as my mother awaited death. As certain as unrequited love and the fragility of holding it altogether. In work, play and home. They're never satisfied. Never will be. It's never enough, what I do. Chain reaction.

Story of my life.

I needed this shit as much as a moose with antlers needs a hat rack on his head.

I thought –

My brother has it all. Always did. The looks, the girlfriends clamouring to date the hockey star, the volleyball captain, the devil-may-care stud. The son who was everything a son could be to his father. And mother. For the most part. Except for some adolescent rebellion. And I know our father vicariously relished in Bruce's teenage displays of male bravado, what with the drinking, the smoking, the fucking, the fighting.

My language meant something to Maman, at least, I told myself. But my desires meant more. Sadly. So much more. A cloud over every accomplishment. A cloud through which the rain never fell. Tears built up. I wouldn't allow myself to cry.

Boys don't cry.

I must accept. Move on. It wasn't in my nature to wallow in these feelings. Was it? Doing so was futile, unmanly. Might as well try capturing all the rain in my open mouth. Or fog in a jar to sell to gullible tourists from the Mainland.

As I've always done.

Move on.

Jackytar

f o u r t e e n

■

Our Fath…who art in heaven,
Hallowed be thy name;
Thy king…dominion come;
Thy will be done on earth as it is in heaven.
Give us this day our daily bread;
And forgive us our debts,
As we forgive our debtors.
And lead us not into temptation, but deliver us from evil;
For thine is the ki…dominion,
And the power and the glory,
For ever. Amen.

f i f t e e n

∎

Night after night, he lay awake wondering. Lay in his bed alone. Touching himself until the explosion of ecstasy provided a moment, just a moment, of pleasure, an illusory feeling, for within seconds he felt more alone than before. Sometimes he drifted off, dreaming strange dreams.

Alex dreamt of frozen ponds, evergreen forests and branches laden with snow, rabbit tracks at their base, and melting snowflakes trickling down the glass pane of the window of his youth.

Because he knew little of love or hate, he was puzzled: Was this what it was supposed to be like?

When he'd first met him, he'd thought he was beautiful, a beauty of both mind and spirit, the perfect blend. So imperious standing there, like the self he'd dreamt of being for so long, the body that he desired, the personality that won others, the presence so coveted.

Even imperfection could be perfect.

Déclic!

Awe. Love at first sight. Desire for this Supreme Being. Eyes so wide and blue. Light brown hair. The best of the best. Somehow pleasing in his totality. None of the awkwardness he knew.

Still knows.

None of the abuse, the othering, the invisibility. Unsoiled and as pure as pure can be in another human being. Sharp intake of breath. This image would never leave his mind.

Remember this ruptured moment.

Forever.

The dream wavered. Then burst.

Déclic!

Replaced by an earlier dream. He was a boy. He donned thigh rubbers, a yellow raincoat and a sou'wester. Playing in the pouring rain, boots covered in muck, for the ground in his yard was soggy as lead. Jumping with delight into potholes on the acne-pocked road. Then springing out. Like jumping on the big rocks in the creek or from ice floe to ice floe in the harbour like a real seal hunter. Like Poppy Murphy used to.

Holding his face up to the streaming waters coming from heaven.

Sticking out his tongue to taste the wet.

He couldn't get enough.

Never could.

Déclic!

Then later again…in a bedroom with a man and two women. On the floor. On the bed. Alex's hand dangled near his hair. He asked himself: Should I?

Time is suspended.

Time is dead.

Time will come again.

He evaluated. The women couldn't see. They couldn't imagine, even, so sure were they of their allure. He couldn't help it, this attraction.

This love!

Alex touched his hair.

So fine.

So lustrous and soft.

Softer than he could have imagined.

Inside him, there were feelings he couldn't explain. And secrets that he could never share, he thought.

He didn't react, did he? No, yes, he didn't protest. Which was a reaction.

Alex was inwardly jubilant, outwardly nonchalant. Content in this stolen moment. The women were unaware, for one of them caressed Alex simultaneously. Her touch was a shadow touch on his shoulder. Her kiss a shadow kiss. Unlike the wetness of the summer shower or the soft deluge of the fall storm Alex relished in his dream. So like the luxury of his friend's soft hair.

The women lingered on the outside of them. Alex was connected and yet apart. Something was happening. Something good and strong and peaceful and unexpected, and Alex suspected that he shared in this wonderment. He felt it deep in his bones as sure as he knew the rain.

He marvelled: How is one ever to know? How can you be sure?

The answer is you cannot.

Jackytar

The moment passed. The evening spun by. An eternity of cherished, clandestine touching. Enough to last a lifetime. And perhaps they must. And frottage with the girls. Interspersed with embarrassed giggles and short comments and quips that they all delighted in. The next day, they crossed each other at noon on the way to the Dining Hall. He was on his way back. Alex was going. They stopped and chatted.

Alex smiled and said he had a good time last night. He didn't know that rain could be so much fun since he was a child.

Suddenly, unexpectedly, out of nowhere, he said: You should be ashamed.

In a soft voice.

Gentle.

Non-threatening.

Alex couldn't even be sure he had heard him correctly, so he said: What? What did you say?

Innocently, as if not knowing, but he knew.

And he said: Never mind. Doesn't matter.

And Alex knew it was true. And they spent the afternoon together. Talking and laughing and sharing yarns of the hometowns, which they both sought to escape, but would carry with them forever.

sixteen

■

Tues*day*

"G'marnin! How's it goin, m'son?" He was wearing his old blue fisherman's tam and nothing suited him better.

"Could be worse," I replied. "I'm not used to getting up so early though."

"Bruce just told me he called the hospital already. No news. She's hangin on. But we better head over there soon just in case."

I poured myself some coffee and got some bread to toast. "I'm surprised Evelyn and Bruce have a wood stove. They seem to like things brand spanking new."

He chuckled. "Nutten like a real fire in the marnin, I spose."

"True and they got the modern stove and appliances, too, I guess. Which one do they use most often?"

"Electric," he said, "but they gits decent use outta the wood stove, too. Especially Bruce. He likes the warmth and makin toast over the fire, just like you. You can take the b'y outta the bay, but ya can't take the bay outta the b'y. There's some hort jam I made in the fridge, if ya wants it? Some bakeapple, too."

"Thanks. I'd love some."

I picked the bottle of blueberry jam out of the fridge door, saving the bakeapple for later, and raised the stove lid with the lifter. A good fire burned. Not too hot. I used the poker to shift the wood around until the embers were perfect.

"So Dad, how are ya feeling about everything?"

He hesitated. "I wish there was somethin more I could do, b'y."

"You've done enough, Dad. You cared for her over the years." I turned the bread over in the wire toaster.

"He-yeah, I s'pose I did all I could do. Twasn't always easy."

"That's for sure," I said.

Maman had been difficult to live with. When she wasn't retreating to her music room or holed up in her bedroom few things we did or said seemed to please her except at Christmas and rare moments she and I shared together talking French or me listening to her organ playing. Meal times were often the site of tension.

Déclic!

"What'd ya do today?" he'd ask her innocently at suppertime, all of us seated at the table.

"Hmmpf!" she'd say with that famous Newfoundland sound of disdain, contempt and frustration. Untranslatable and untranscribable. "Same ole thing. Muckin around in ere. Practised some hymns."

"Sure why don't ya come wid me fer a walk after supper, France? Let's mosey down to Shepherd's Bluff? We can stop in on Louise and Charlie if ya wants?"

"I ave a headache. You go. They're your friends," she'd say spitefully.

DOUGLAS GOSSE

"They'd be your friends, too, France, if you gave it a shot."

And then it would go from bad to worse. She'd storm off. She took to having most of her meals alone, up in her bedroom or in her music room, creeping into the kitchen like a ghost after she thought we'd all left. Sometimes, I'd bring her a plate myself.

"*Mon garçon est un garçon*," she'd lamely joke, time after time again, forcing a brief smile.

I put the finished slice in the oven to keep warm and started another. "Dad, do ya want a slice?"

"No, thank you. I had enough. Thanks." He finished sipping his tea and put the cup in the dishwasher.

"Dad, can you sit for a minute?"

"Sure, I spose I can do that. We can't leave anyhow until youse is all ready. Bruce and Evelyn are still rushin about."

"Great! I'd like you to continue where you finished off yesterday, I mean, if you don't mind?"

He raised his eyebrows, inhaled sharply and then nodded, "spose it wouldn't hurt. Might even do some good." He took a fresh cup from the cupboard, poured himself another cup of tea, mixed in milk and sugar, and plonked himself down on the chair. "Now where was I, Alex, m'son?"

"You were telling me all about your trip to see Maman's family. What happened afterwards, Dad?"

"Ahh, yis! I'll give ya the shortened version." He winked. "We were in the gravel pit just outside the town where she grew ap. We stayed there and talked for what

Jackytar

seemed like hours. After she quieted down, she told me her mudder was religious and had called her a whore – putain was the word she used, for not marryin in a Roman Cat'lic church. Sheer blasphemy she called it, accordin to yer mudder. That she was goin to hell for all eternity and her children, too, or bastards as yer grandmudder called youse.

"Well, yer mudder swore that she'd never go back there no mar! She was in good spirits first. She said how good our marriage was. How she longed to see youse again in Bond Cove."

"I see," I said, keeping my questions to myself. He took another sip of the tea, slurping loudly and continued while I ate my toast.

"Did you know yer mudder and I met at the Officer's Club?"

I shook my head.

"She was in the adjacent yard, hangin up clothes. She looked some sweet there in her cotton smock and starched apron. I wasn't sure if she was the woman a the house or no, but I had to find out. It helped that we'd had a few drinks and the b'ys bugged me to go over. I was a bit timid but they told me I was a good-lookin enough chap in them days."

He still was, I observed. Although sixty-six, he looked ten years younger. While his brow was furrowed from being outside in the sun and salty air, and he suffered from asthma and arthritis, his build remained powerful and solid. Bruce was his spitting image. I, on the other hand, had the stocky frame and aquiline nose of some of the mixed-race Jackytars that I used to recognize in passing in St. John's. I also used to know several who were in education and health care, or worked for the government. In Toronto, the only Natives or part-Natives I saw regularly were homeless.

Did they see me as Native too, I wondered for the umpteenth time? Or did they see me as a white man?

Dad poured the remainder of his tea into the saucer to cool it.

"So after we returned home from the Port-au-Port Peninsula, she was awright for a time. Then things started goin downhill fast. She quit her part-time job as a maid," he explained. "No explanation, cept she said she was tired, while I was workin all these extra hours tryin to pay for the little bungalow we were rentin on Pleasant Street. Busy as a nailer, I was!

"I worked in the shipyard as a clerk. Worked lotsa shifts on the army base, too, to make ends meet. I'd come home in the evenin and the place would be in shambles, dirty dishes, magazines on the floor, sheet music lyin around everywhere, and the damned tube blarin! The pump argan sat in a corner, unused, coated in dust. She wouldn't go near the thing. Funny, eh? We'd have a horrible time arg'in and sometimes I thought I'd lose it and punch her lights out. Course I never did. But the worse," he stopped to take a deep breathe, "the worse was how she treated youse! Dirty diapers, half-starved and she lyin on the couch. You don't remember that, I spose, do ya?"

"Nope."

Déclic!

But a memory surfaced. Maman dozing on the couch, shooing me away when I tried to rouse her. Bruce a baby. Red faced from cryin. Me trying to feed him some cereal with milk that he pawed away. I was a small child.

Jackytar

"So what happened?" I said.

"Well, I hated to yank ya outta French immersion but I bundled youse up and carted ye out to Bond Cove. Only fer yer grandmudder and grandfadder, I dunno what I would a done. Or what would a become a youse. You owes them yer life. For sure as Oi'm sittin here today! We would a been in dire straights wid'out their help rearin you b'ys ap through the years."

Déclic!

I recalled my grandmother's smiling face. A large woman, she was most often in the kitchen, cooking and baking for the bed and breakfast guests, especially during the warmer months. During the winter when times were less rushed, she knitted sweaters, mittens, scarves, and woollen hats. Enough for an army. Once we'd all been appropriately outfitted, she'd donate the leftovers to St. Stephen's Anglican Church. She was a kindly woman, a gentle soul and Dad turned after her more than he did Poppy Murphy. When I was out of school for sickness or on holiday I used to love watching her afternoon soaps with her on the television in the living room.

"My oh my," she'd say, pointing at the melodramatics of some actor, "I can't believe that one there! She poisoned her husband and now she's trying to break up the marriage of that other couple, too. She's a devil, that one! Tsk! Tsk!"

I was never fully convinced she knew they were actors and not real, or that she really understood the plots. She never seemed to get the names of the characters straight, perhaps because she knitted while she watched, and tended to talk with me a lot, too, during advertisements. Then again, she read the Bible nightly, too and I wasn't sure how well she understood those stories either, with her primary school education. Her stories were a part of her daily routine for most of her adult life. If ever she missed them, she'd ache to see them the next day

"Nanny was a good woman," I said, "and Poppy Murphy tended to us a lot, too."

"They sure did!" He became stern. "Can I tell ya somethin and promise ya won't ever repeat it, okay?"

"I promise I won't tell a soul."

He whispered. "Twas so bad, I had to git her to a doctor. That was the first time. They locked her up…in the mental. Ya never knowed that, did ya, Alex?"

I swallowed. "I suspected."

"Two whole weeks. Clinically depressed, they said. A danger to herself and to youse. We didn't know about such things back then like we do today," he added apologetically.

"Well, now it's on the television all the time," I said.

"He-yeah, back then, no one ever used to talk about depression. You'd be ashamed to mention yer nerves was bad." He straightened up in his chair and spoke with pride. "Ever since then, though, I saw to it that your mudder was always under a doctor's care and takin her medication. And she had her ups and downs, Lard knows. More downs than up."

"Which doctor treated her?" I asked, but knew the answer.

"Oh, Dr. Lowry. He was a good doctor, that man. A saint in these parts. Did everything from deliverin babies to treatin people for cancer. And cases like yer mudder."

Jackytar

"Dad, when did Dr. Lowry pass away?"

"Oh, a few year ago."

"And who was Maman's doctor after that?"

"Oh, she had this one and that, up at the clinic. They come and go. But she's had the same one now for a few year. Dr. Singh. A nice fellow from up yer way. Toronto, I think. He's some good, b'y."

Dr. Lowry had been the main doctor here since before we moved to Bond Cove. He had seemed an old man to me even then. Maman's transformation had occurred about the same time he passed away and she would have switched doctors. Could she have been improperly medicated all those years?!

"Ya know, when yer mudder moved here, she was still some fine piece a stock! She had this beautiful long hair back in them days. Black and silky. Flowed down her back almost to er waist."

"What happened to it? I can only remember it being short."

"Yer grandfadder put the kibosh on that first we moved back to Bond Cove. He joked one day about her lookin like Pocahontas. She cut it all off wid scissors that very evenin." He shook his head and bit his lip. "Her hair looked like a birch broom in the fits. My, twas it ever shockin! The next marnin, I tookt her over to Maisy's Salon to git a proper haircut. I begged her to let it grow out again but she never would. She could be so stubborn, yer mudder."

He stood.

Déclic!

It's easy to love the dead and dying when they can't

respond anymore, I thought. The living, too, when they're silent and miles or oceans away. I pondered Maman's medication and her zombie-like state through the decades but said nothing.

There was nothing left to say.

Jackytar

seventeen

■

The grey-white walls were also yellowish. An unpleasant yellow. The look of decay. Matching her sickly pallor. Shuffling in the corridor was the same old gentleman in his plaid bathrobe and green cotton pyjamas, his drooling mouth muttering obscurely. He stuck out, this gentleman, who had once been a policeman, city councillor, janitor, or miner. Rich man, poor man, beggar man, thief. They're all alike. His slippers were blue and grimy. Tufts of hair sprouted from his ears and nose. More than decorated his head. There weren't many men there. All dead. Plenty of widows, though.

A sage perhaps? An idiot savant? One of Shakespeare's wise fools?

I almost stopped to listen to his words. To speak with him. To plead for grains of wisdom. Surely someone so aged must have many to share. But then I reconsidered and walked past him. No time for sages today. I was perhaps the only fool. Nurses walked around I knew, but not because

I could hear their rubber-soled shoes. No. Because I sometimes heard their stage whispers as they consoled the dying, sponge bathed them, adjusted ventilators, and prodded them with needles.

There was a sign: All Visitors Please Check In.

So we did. First I printed my name in capital letters in blue ink. Then I signed the lined page of the book and wrote down the date. Patients and visitors. We were no longer loved ones - sons, daughters, husbands, wives, brothers, sisters, aunts, uncles, cousins, and friends, but visitors. Death had levelled us. The medical institution had given us a role to play and we had grown up seeing death for entertainment all our lives. The script was written. Television and movies and literature had taught us well. None of my blood kin would tear out their hair, gnash their teeth, or howl with crazy grief. Too dignified for that. Too male.

Society's expectations and policing had beaten public sentiment out of them.

Sensation Sensei. Emotion(less) Enforcers. Passion Police.

Despite Dad's maudlin display earlier, I knew he'd keep a stiff upper lip.

Déclic!

Jackytar

I think –

Society needs you to be stoic, to work yourselves
into an early grave. Shhh! Don't complain.
Drink.
Drug yourself.
Fuck, adulterers!
Eat fatty junk foods and marbled beef to heart
disease and cancers.
But do it quietly, slowly…Shhh!
Creep towards your grave and remember, above
all else, when you're alone and drunk, vomiting, drugged,
and rotting from cancer,
or AIDS
as your heart stops beating:
You are victimizers.
You are brutes.
Shh!
Your role is to marry.
Inseminate.
Work.
And work.
And then work some more, until you wear out
and die early.
Do it without a moan, groan, or protestation.
Be lucky you're tolerated at all.
Chauvinist pigs.
Perform your manliness. Your manhood.
Sparks of testosterone and chunks of willpower
will fizzle,
and then die,
and you will draw your last breath,

and they will weep and place large
pennies on your eyes for
you to give to Charon,
for your passage to the Underworld on
the river Styx,
saving the bills for themselves.
And you will have been a man

in
brief
moments.

Jackytar

e i g h t e e n

■

"*C'est toi, hein? Est-ce bien toi, Maman?*" she said.

Maman was delirious. Asking for her mother. The Francophone grandmother I'd never known. Weak as a kitten. Frantic to communicate. She looked at me with cloudy brown eyes. At them. But she didn't see us. She saw ghosts from the past. Dead people. Waiting for her, no doubt. Beckoning her to come into the light. Into oblivion.

Or eternal life.

She laughed. A horrible strangled stream of laughter. She'd never laughed in life, but she laughed in death. Released from the prisons of her lifelong melancholia.

It was ugly.

Yet, there was a grisly beauty there. She had taken on the air of a saint. A sufferer. A dignity she never felt in life infiltrated her features in death. Her strangled voice was like the voice of a shaman. We listened, ears cocked, as if awaiting divine words. And then she sang, her voice pure and thin.

"Lo he comes the voice of angels, singing softly, singing Lord."

I couldn't bear it.

"She's on her way out," mumbled Dad, stroking her right hand. "Hold her hand, m'son. Hold yer mudder's hand for the last time."

I reacted but it was too late. Bruce already held her other lovely hand, the left one, with its long tapered fingers, in his Viking grip. I laid mine to rest on her shoulder instead, as softly as a blue jay lighting on a leaf and with my other hand I caressed her grey-black Indian hair that she had shorn off in a fit of rage eons ago and never allowed to grow back.

She spoke.

"*Chut! Chut! Dis-moi, tu vas la retrouver mon p'tit. Fils prodigue. Pauvre p'tit bébé. Fragile, frêle. God love us and save us.*"

She clutched her small golden locket. Inside, I knew, was a small framed picture of a cherub. The necklace never left her neck, even as she lay dying.

I was nearest her choked whispers, her choked singing.

They nodded unknowingly, but me –

I listened.

I felt what she felt. The room so silent. Time suspended by her dying. Autumn, chilly and damp, has been denied entry to this death chamber. Death, hot and dry and un-fresh, was keeping it at bay.

Her voice progressively weakened, like an echo in the mountains. It had been like this since we got here. As soon as they called us. Told us to hurry up and get over. "She's waning," they said.

Like the sunlight in the mid-afternoon. Waning.

*J*ackytar

"*P'tit Alexandre, tu vas la trouver…ma cassette…ma chanson?*"

My ears peaked. She really recognized me. Me, the prodigal son. Looked me in the eyes. Lucid eyes. No longer faded and confused.

Sharp for an instant.

"*Quoi ça, Maman? De quoi tu parles?*" I asked.

"*La cassette que j'ai faite. Faut pas qu'ils la trouvent.*" Then she looked away, or rather her lucidity went away, for her eyes still looked in my general direction. And she sang –

"Lo, he comes the voice of angels, singing softly, singing Lord."

Suddenly, she fixed on Bruce and then Dad, as if startled. Like a rabbit caught live in a snare, about to get hit on the back of the head with the brunt of a hatchet. She knew.

No, I was mistaken.

Rather, she looked past them, past her husband and youngest son. The blonde ones.

Slow motion.

Déclic!

A moment of rupture, dragging on interminably. I noted her husband's blondness and her son's similarity to him – the spitting image.

Clarity.

I saw none of me in them. Nor them in me. Not in her husband, not in her son. They were freakishly healthy, huge and powerful looking in this room where the sick pass on.

Wait. Bruce's eyes were wide and I began to imagine a sign of our Indian ancestors there around the

DOUGLAS GOSSE

ever-so-slightly-hooded pale blue eyes. In the turn of the eyelid.

I realized –

We can't ever totally escape the legacy of our bodies.

And this shocked me, for some reason.

Bruce had withdrawn his hand. Stood bewildered. Her hand was dry. Dry and withering. I'd never touch it again while she was alive I realized, so I greedily squeezed it one last time.

Dad…mouth mirthless, drooping at the corners. Eyes shrouded.

They won't cry, will they?

Tears coursed freely down my cheeks, man-woman that I am.

Hermaphrodite.

That we all are.

"Frenchie, me love. I loves ya. I do. I loves ya, m'ducky." He lifted her hand and kissed it, his voice breaking pitiably. "Fren…Frennchie?"

Her eyes closed.

Truly like a flame being extinguished. Or a light switch being turned off.

Déclic!

And she was gone.

Jackytar

n i n e t e e n

■

Dr. Dobbin and the nurse did some paper work. Dad called the undertaker. Within mere minutes, they'd taken her body.

Lickety split.

Older outport dwellers might neglect wills, but deaths were planned down to the last detail. Lives were harder to control. Less so death.

Can't keep permourning, i.e. performing mourning. Get er ap and ready fer tonight!

Twas one of the few breaks from monotony…after all.

t w e n t y
∎

Mid-morning. Evelyn buzzed around the house. Bruce too. Getting ready for the trip to Bond Cove. I was packed, having just brought my backpack. Everything had been arranged. I was surprised that Dad had taken care of all arrangements in advance.

"Yes, b'y, ya gotta take care of all that stuff, right?" he told me. Questions aren't always questions, but affirmations. Comments. Reached decisions. Lip service.

She would be buried in Bond Cove, in St. Stephen's Anglican Cemetery. No Roman Catholic priest would be present but an Anglican minister instead, an extremely obese woman who "…loves fried chicken and children. And she's single."

This I was told by Evelyn, who claimed to know her well. The minister's fatness, femaleness and singleness made her an item of curiosity in Bond Cove.

Respected yet odd.

"Her name's Rev. Heather Byrne, a funny name for a priest, and she's an angel, too, despite her name. No pun intended." Evelyn's sense of irony surfaced from time to time. "You just wait and see. She'll conduct an amazing service."

I emptied the dishwasher. Everything was spiffy and polished and mechanized. Push a button and dirty dishes are cleansed. Push another and dirty clothes are washed. Push another and food is delivered to the house or a cab arrives at the door within minutes. Push another music fills the comfy family room. The gas fireplace springs to life with yet another button. Life is a matter of pushing buttons and instantaneous gratification. More time for talking and building relationships, I supposed, wondering how these sophisticated townies must perceive Bond Cove.

Quaint and rustic?

Evelyn buzzed around, excited over the drama of death. Her voice was elevated and her colour high. What an adventure to set out mid-week early in the afternoon to Bond Cove. All the food and nice clothes and visitors and gossip and eating.

I looked forward to it, too.

"Bruce, have you emptied the garbage yet?" Evelyn yelled from upstairs.

"Oi'm gettin the car ready. Hold on to yer jigger!"

"It needs to be done before we leave! I told you that!" she insisted, muttering something about not having a jigger.

He dropped whatever he was doing and stormed into the kitchen a minute later to empty the garbage.

"Bruce, I'll do that," I said.

"Thanks, Alex. Jaysus!" he rolled his eyes towards the upstairs.

"Bruce, by the way, did Maman keep tapes around

Torbay House anywhere?"

He paused. "He-yeah, in her music room. We got her a good quality tape recorder the other year. She has piles of em in her office. Spent hours listening to em. Recordin her own music at the church, too. Why? Is that what she was mumblin to ya about in French before she…passed away?"

"Bruce, the garbage emptied yet?" screamed Evelyn.

Bruce left the kitchen and ran up the stairs to confront her.

For the time being, I decided to keep Maman's final request a secret between Maman and me, a parting gesture of her trust. At least, that's what I wanted to believe. I wanted to construct my own meaning, my own reality, and interpret her trust as a bridge between the years of silence because I was gay and a sinner.

Jackytar

twenty
one

■

Before we left St. John's, I lay down on the cot for a few minutes and closed my eyes. I longed to see Torbay House, our home, named in honour of the land our ancestors had come from in Devon, England. Poppy Murphy built the house just prior to the Great Depression, which had little impact on many rural Newfoundlanders anyway. It was a Victorian house built on top of what quickly became baptized Murphy's Hill. Poppy Murphy had been a sea captain. Made his mark leading seal hunts and fishing for cod. He made good money during Prohibition, too, running illegal wine and spirits off the nearby French islands of St. Pierre et Miquelon, the same islands where I'd been an exchange student for several months as a teenager and gained firsthand exposure to French culture.

When I was a boy, he'd confided, "Several times we had to dump rum over the sides of the boat when the Coast Guard's lights shone upon us! But they never caught us, no siree, Bob!"

He drank most of his money and spent a good portion

on women. Skipper Murph, as he was known, was reputed to have scores of children up and down the coasts of Newfoundland and Labrador. Mixed-race children. He hid nothing about his fondness for Native women. He never spoke about it in Nanny's presence, of course, but anywhere else was fair game.

Déclic!

"They're quite pretty when they're young," he'd brag. "Curvy and smooth skinned, with long black hair. My son, look out! But when they gits to be about twenty-five or so! Lard sufferin Christ! Their teeth falls out and they gits as big as whales. Poor diet, I spose. Always eatin junk food. Smokin and drinkin. No dentists up there for that lot. Nutten uglier than a toothless woman. Some a those mixed-race children tends to be pretty lookin, too, wid blue eyes. Light-coloured hair lots a times."

My hair was as dark as night. Like an Indian's. Like hers.

There was even a popular song about my grandfather's tragic death, often sung at times to the accompaniment of the fiddle, accordion and spoons:

'Skipper Murph & The Bona Vister'

Tall are the tales of Newfoundlanders on the sea,
And Skipper Murph's were the tallest you ever
did see.
He sailed upon the Bona Vister,
A better cap'n did never exist, sir!
Ahoy, ahoy, de diddle di deh

Jackytar

In March he set sail upon a Friday morn,
Despite the warnings and the Irishmen's scorn,
The Bona Vister was a great big rig,
He said: the bigger the better in order to jig!
Ahoy, ahoy, de diddle di deh

The sea was churning and what a sight!
He made them fish all day and night.
The next marning was foggy and dark and dim,
When the Bona Vister hit upon a mountain a sin.
Ahoy, ahoy, de diddle di deh

The men was worried and some panicked, too,
For in the skiffs was room for only twenty-two.
But Skipper Murph, o he kept his calm,
He radioed for help and read em a psalm.
Ahoy, ahoy, de diddle di deh

So they lowered the skiffs into the sea,
And filled her with the young and free.
Skipper Murph and the rest they climbed ashore,
Except the shore was a block a ice afore.
Ahoy, ahoy, de diddle di deh

And Skipper Murph they found at last,
He and his men were frozen fast,
There was Pierce and Tucker and Johnny Reid,
There was Sharp and Critch and Austin Mead.
Ahoy, ahoy, de diddle di deh

But Skipper Murph, he was standing tall,
His hands on his Bible, he would never fall,
His grip was fierce and ever so strong,
That even in death he'd never been wrong!
Ahoy, ahoy, de diddle di deh

DOUGLAS GOSSE

Yes, tall are the tales of Newfoundlanders on the
sea,
But the moral of this yarn is plain to see –
Don't ye ever sail on a Friday morn,
For if ye does, ye'll never return!
Ahoy, ahoy, de diddle di deh.

Evelyn called out from the landing of the stairs, "Alex,
we're almost ready to go!"

I opened my eyes.

"Be there in a minute!" I shouted back.

Cursed.

We were all cursed, those who built our lives around
the whims of the Atlantic Ocean. Their luggage was
piled up in the porch. Evelyn and Bruce scurried
around, talking in heated stage whispers, making sure
they'd forgotten nothing.

The Trans-Canada Highway was foggy. No surprise
there. One hundred and twenty-one days of fog per year;
the most in Canada. Fog was my sunshine. The Avalon
Peninsula, seen from the highway, gave the impression
of an unsoiled land, yet to be discovered, with this
incongruous highway arising out of nowhere. We
seemed to drive through different ecosystems as we left
town. From lush hills and ponds left and right, to flatter
and marshier land as far as the eye could see. Then back
again. How unlike this was from downtown Toronto,
where aggressive drivers made crossing the street
dangerous, beggars clamoured for spare change and dirty
concrete and tall buildings replaced nature. Yet, I preferred
the safety and anonymity of Toronto.

Nostalgia is like that.

Jackytar

Automatic pilot. I had driven this route thousands of times. The traffic was light, mostly heading towards St. John's, not away. Cottagers and baymen heading back to town for another week. Students going back to post-secondary colleges and university. Out of high school, I had opted for the Newfoundland University of Language and Culture for my undergraduate degree. Whereas most Canadian universities' second language departments persisted with outdated programs that sought to prepare their students for literary study, my program focussed on language acquisition and cultural learning. For the first time in my life, being a Jackytar was a blessing.

Déclic!

"Hey, at some universities, professors don't even know French is spoken outside Quebec, let alone in Newfoundland," said a senior student my first week in the common room, "but the instructors here are well versed in Francophone Newfoundland language and culture. You must meet Geneviève Benoit. Doctoral student and instructor. You'll like her."

And I did. Long straight black hair like my mother's must have been as a young girl and brown eyes. She had a slight French accent when she spoke English. We proceeded to give seminars together on Franco-Newfoundland history, music and language. One day, the beginning of first semester, she took me by the hand and directed me towards the mirror in the common room.

Elle demande: *Que vois-tu*? *Qui vois-tu*?

I stared at my dark skin, hair and eyes, the strong nose, somewhat bulbous at the end, the thick neck.

Je bégaye et finis par répondre: *Ben, je me vois. Je vois moi-même. Juste un gars.* Alexandre Murphy.

Elle insiste: Non! Regarde de plus près!

She took the back of my head and forced me to peer closer.

Regarde ça, donc! C'est toi ça dans le miroir. C'est pas un blanc. Toi, t'es Franco-Terre-Neuvien. T'es pas blanc. Rappelle-toi de ton histoire, de notre histoire, et ne renie plus jamais ton sang!

From that moment onward, I saw myself differently. I was a Jackytar, and so was Geneviève Benoit.

"Watch out for the moose, eh?" said Bruce, bringing me back to the present.

"Don't worry," I said.

"Alex, how's Keith doing by the way?" asked Evelyn. This was the first mention of my partner by any of them.

"I need to call him later," I said. "Think my cell phone will work in Bond Cove?"

"Hard to say," said Evelyn. "Touch and go, but your father has a landline."

"So how is the Bay Street capt'n a industry doin these days? Still rakin in the dough, I spose?" said my brother.

I didn't know if Bruce resented Keith's success or that he was gay, or both.

"Alright. He's doing fine. Busy as usual. Working his ass off." I turned on an easy listening station. "She's gone, eh? You're gonna miss her, eh, Dad?"

"I will," he said. "That I will."

"Here today, gone tomorrow," said Evelyn. "You just never know, now, do you?"

"Yup, tis hard to believe!" responded Bruce, in a bizarre tone again. I sized him up out of my peripheral vision. He

Jackytar

had skilfully contorted his six-foot four body into the seat. He wore an expensive sweater, jeans and a trendy pair of black leather hiking boots. His haircut was spiky and artfully gelled and I suspected he had Scandinavian highlights.

He's a bloody metrosexual, I mused.

"Yeah, at least she didn't suffer too long," I said, self-consciously adding to the clichés I normally detested.

Bruce bristled in his seat. "Whattaya mean?" he demanded.

I used my best teacher's voice, firm yet friendly, slightly authoritarian. "I mean thankfully she was sick for only the past month. And it was really only the past week that things became so awful. I'm just glad it was over quick, that's all."

"Geez, ya gotta be kiddin!"

I was no longer on automatic pilot. I peered intently through the fog as if at any moment we might hit the proverbial moose, our car would spin, roll and then we'd careen into a ditch. There was an unreal quality to this scenario. I turned the music down.

"Explain."

One word.

"Jaysus, brudder. Where ya been to? Ya knows Mudder's been half off her head her entire life! Whattaya mean about it being quick? She's been dying for half a century already! We here had to put up wid it, while you was up in Toronto and traipsing around the globe! Hmmpf!"

"Now b'ys!" intervened Dad. "Give it a rest. Yer mudder's not even cold. I won't have any arg'in today."

In the rear view mirror, I saw Evelyn tap Bruce on his

shoulder. "Listen, emotions are running high. Let's try and relax, okay? We're almost there."

"*D'accord*," I said simply. "I'm not getting into this. Maman's dead. It's not the time."

Bruce turned his head towards the window as I turned off the highway. Just a few more minutes to endure. The foliage became different. Bog and stunted trees. There were little communities peppered about that you'd miss if you blinked, an on-going joke in this region. Sheep dotted some of the rocky hills. Duos or trios of children in brightly coloured parkas, with matching home knit hats and mittens, walked along the shoulder of the road, on their way to a friend's house to play and watch television.

I said no more, but in my mind I wanted to pull the car over and shout –

You little fool!

Always thinking of yourself first!

Never considering other people's feelings, least of which your family's.

You never could get past the glory of being you!

You still don't have the sense of a louse!

Golden Boy.

Star athlete.

And look at you now.

Yuppie wannabe.

A clone.

You useless inarticulate piece of shit!

Jackytar

You with your
   little teacher wifey,
      your big house,
   your mall clothes and expensive haircut.

   No individuality.
Just going through the motions.
      Some things never change.
You're no different now than when we were kids.

   I fucking hate you,
you miserable piece of homophobic,
   self-absorbed trash.
      Get it into your big,
   stupid
blonde head
   that it's not always about you,
      buster!

   Déclic!
   And then I realized: I'm not a saint!
   Alex Murphy is not a saint. I may be expected to be
twice as good, to show em all that I'm up to speed, that I
can cut the mustard. I may be unusually pious and good to
compensate for my sexuality, for my non-whiteness, for my
right to belong. But there's one thing I can do almost as
well as loving, as well as anyone else.
   In brief moments, I allow myself to hate.
   They usually don't last very long.

t w e n t y
t w o

■

Have you ever been into an Irishman's shanty?
The water is scarce, the whiskey is plenty,
A three-legged stool, a table to match,
A stick in the door, instead of a latch.

– Irish Newfoundland ditty, author unknown

twenty
three

■

I looked up at Torbay House and felt that tingling sense of coming home. It was expensive to maintain such a large house, but fortunately Dad managed. He'd mortgaged the house when Bruce and I were children. With the money, he'd fixed the roof, installed up-to-date plumbing and wiring and set up Torbay House as a bed and breakfast.

"You'd be surprised what a bit a paint and glue can do, eh?" said Dad, his pride evident. Bruce ignored us, his spite replaced with cold calm as we unpacked the car.

"You can say that again!" I said. Torbay House was painted a vibrant and dignified white that glowed softly. Crisp wooden shutters adorned the windows on both floors and glistening French doors beautified the front parlour. "It's never looked better."

My joy changed to gloom upon entering the old Victorian. No more Maman to emerge from her sanctuary off the main hallway, all surprised. She was probably being driven to the funeral home in the hearse as we spoke.

"The hallway looks marvellous," I said, trying to keep

our spirits up. Indeed, silver and gold garland were draped over the grandfather clock and taped up high on the walls. A bright red and white doily covered the telephone table.

"He-yeah, we did that up last summer. Bruce and I did the planching. We got the old grandfadder clock tuned up in St. John's, too. Not bad, eh, for an ole fogey?"

The new oak floor shone with wax. The walls were a pearly colour that set them off to perfection. The grandfather clock was keeping time properly for the first time in years.

"Yer mudder didn't have nutten to do wid it," Dad said. "We did it all by ourselves. Bruce and me. Every last lick a work." He looked towards the decorations. "Now she did put that up before she got too sick."

"Dad, do people still come here to snap pictures?"

"He-yeah, indeed they do! From all over the island and the Mainland. Some from the United States and Germany. They still raps at our door now and then and asks fer a tour like they used to when you was a b'y. Lotsa Germans buyin property around here these days. Loves it, they do. They likes the old houses and bein by the sea. The woods and the lakes and ponds. The water. Nature. We got it all here, b'y."

Evelyn ran upstairs to the bathroom, claiming an emergency. We finished bringing the luggage in ourselves. I paused in the hallway. There it was again − Maman's music room. A festive Christmas wreath was pinned to the door, incongruous given the circumstances. Sometimes during Christmas, she'd invite me in to share some of the bakeapple jam she greedily guarded. She'd pick the golden bakeapples herself on the Bond Cove marshes every July and boil them down to make jam. It was her only claim to

Jackytar

domestic indulgence in the expansive kitchen that many would have tremendously enjoyed. She'd tormented Dad until he'd installed a little sink and toilet off her music room in what used to be a large linen closet. Her world of music and imagination had been more real to her than we were.

After unpacking, I went to the kitchen to boil water for a cup of tea. I was sizing up the contents of the cupboards when Dad entered.

"Hello, there," he greeted, his face ruddy from the chilly night air. "Just got off the phone and went for a wee walk around the yard. They got her out of town an hour ago. She down at Barnes' Funeral Home. She'll be ready in a few hours. She's the only one they got over there now. We can go see er around 7:00 or 8:00 p.m."

"Glad to hear it," I said.

He sat down and looked towards the woodstove. "Ya got the fire going alright, have ya?"

A modern chrome stove sat ignored alongside a fancy dishwasher. "Tea tastes much better cooked over the fire," I said. "There was a some lovely kindling in the woodbox in the porch. Nice junks of birch wood, too. So I got her going good. You've been busy in the woods, eh?"

He looked a bit sheepish and scratched the back of his head. "Twasn't me who done it. I paid one a them Dobbin boys for a few yaffels a wood. Just as cheap, I reckon. Goin in the woods takes its toll. Me asthma's actin up, especially this time a year in the woods when it's gettin colder."

"Right on. Just as cheap, eh? Only a few dollars." I paused. "So how are ya feeling?"

"Well, I guess it was bound to happen. Either she or I

DOUGLAS GOSSE

had to go first. And she turned out to be the first to kick the bucket. Ya never knows. I'd like to say yer mudder had a good life, but that's pretty much bullshit and you knows it as well as I do, right?"

The kettle started to whistle and I poured the tea.

"So I did the best I could. Kept the place goin. Tookt in guests to help pay for the upkeep and repairs. Kept it all up, b'y! Sometimes I thinks I was as foolish as a caplin." He looked around grimly. "The place looks pretty damn good, though, if I do say so m'self. We fixed up her music room and bathroom again three or four summers ago. She enjoyed that. Plastered and painted. New flooring. Did what we could for her, I spose."

I looked out over the community of about eight hundred, more during the summer. Each small, lit house was filled with its own yarns and secrets. We sipped our milky tea from the big mugs in silence. What else could he have done, indeed?

Jackytar

twenty four

■

A few local women dropped off dishes so we didn't have to bother with cooking. After a late supper of cold plates, we took our time drinking our tea. It was getting dark. Rain threatened to fall. A symphony of screeching birds filled the air. Stearins, small ocean birds on the coast of Newfoundland, joined their larger gull cousins scavenging for fish guts and fish heads thrown off the Government Wharf. The stearins were even more frenzied than the gulls, who'd eat just about anything. As I drove down the hill along the harbour, I watched the stearins hover, dart down to snatch a morsel of fish, then speed off into the air to perch on some distant rock or craggy cliff. Individual wharves dotted the harbour and men wearing navy blue tams and workman's overalls chatted and chewed baccy near flakes where splayed fish were spread to dry. I saw one old skipper spit black juice on the gravel.

Déclic!
"Don't ya be dawdling now, b'y." He spat baccy juice

on the sawdust floor. "Hand me that stick there for the woodharse, luh!"

We were in the store. Netting, jiggers, half-full pails of paint, and buckets filled with rusty nails, bolts and screws lay helter skelter against walls and on shelves. I saw the manual lawn mower, parts of a boat engine and then the sickle for cutting grass. I liked to fool around with the sickle when Poppy Murphy wasn't looking. Next to it was a mound of sticks of wood. He'd cut them on the South Shore and lugged them back in his dory by issself.

I resented helping him when my friends were going up Shepherd's Creek in a dingy. I loosened my grip so the bucksaw would slip a little.

"Jaysus, Alex! Hold er steady, now m'son." He shook his head and sawed with renewed gusto. The ole bucksaw gleamed and smelled because he cleaned it with ile to keep it rust free. Junks of wood fell into the sawdust on the floor, like twas no effort a'tol. I grudgingly wished I could cut wood half as good.

"When I was your age, I had to do all this by m'self," he told me for the thousandth time. The doors were wide open. He glanced towards the *oeil de bœuf* window in Maman's music room. "Fraance! Jaysus Christ! I hates to say it, m'son, but yer mudder's too Injun for er own good. I hopes ye all don't take after her later on in life!"

My grip on the stick tightened.

"Yessir, I hates to say it but tis true. I idden proud of it but I knowed lotsa Injun women in me time, from the Labrador and from yer mudder's carner, too, on the Port-au-Port." He had a habit of sticking out the edge of his tongue in concentration as he sawed, as if biting it. "Don't git me wrong! Lots of em is right good women.

Jackytar

Clean and smart. Christian. Hard workin. But yer mudder," he halted and put more baccy in his cheek, "she idden very ambitious and ambition, m'son, is what got them folks in a kitl a trouble!"

My ears reddened. Junks of stove size wood descended to the floor as if in slow motion, one after another, like feathers. Suddenly, I hated his guts and the emotion of hate was as foreign to me as the sense of acute shame rising from deep within. I'd never felt these dizzying emotions before and I'd never hated him. Feared him a bit, yes, respected him, yes, but never hate. I felt bewildered and embarrassed by this hungry hate, this sickening shame that burned so hotly in my body and the fact that he seemed unaware.

My hands dropped away from the stick as if scalded.

I hope he'll cut his hand off, I thought, but he recovered quickly.

"Christ, Alex, m'son, hold on to the friggin woodharse like I told ya to!"

Silently, I did as I was told. He continued his tirade. "This marning again, she be in that cursed room, playin away at that friggin Lard Sufferin Jaysus pump argan. Like twas all needed to be done round the house." He glanced at my hands, checking to see if I was holding the stick properly. "Yer poor fadder, he don't stop a friggin minute, doin his work and hers, too. Workin his fingers to the bone, that man. He's worn out. Doin yer grandmudder's work, too, since she went on to greener pastures. Work that France should've took over." He looked at me intently. "Oi'm glad youse is here, outta the city. I likes havin m'son and me grandsons here, but Oi'm goin out on the ice again soon."

He shook his head and spat.

"I spoke to her this marnin. Saucy as a crackie, that one. By the Jaysus, I never saw no one like her in all me life. Lazy as a cut dog! Told me she wasn't feelin good and had to take a nap. Scurried off like a jackrabbit into her hole!"

He pulled the stick roughly. I barely avoided scraping my hands up on the rough bark and sharp knots. "Careful, b'y!"

"I am," I said.

"Watch out or ya'll end up wid bandages on yer gaffers. Want some gloves?"

"Nope."

"I tole yer fadder not to do up a friggin music room for her, yessir, I did. But did he listen? No sirree, Bob, he didn't. T'will be the ruin of un. They're all right for a bit a fun," he wagged his index finger at me, "but don't marry em!"

A blistering red heat spread from my ears to my neck, travelling downwards to my chest, where my racing heart threatened to explode. I handed him another stick. He sawed away, his horny knuckles white with force. Twas dead silent in the store. No waves lapping in the landwash. No gulls shrieking. No crows squawking. No stearins screeching. No men chitchatting, swearing and spitting tobacco. No women shouting at each other from the landings of their houses. Just his thundering voice in my ears and my pounding heartbeat.

"A proper woman would be up gettin dinner ready. Poundin away on that ole pump argan. Hear it? Jaysus, what nonsense!"

The sawdust fell to the floor beneath the woodhorse in

Jackytar

a crescendo, piling up like dirty, yellowed snowflakes. His breath shortened.

"Don't you ever become like her, ya hear me? Yer fadder's white, so youse is white, too. You'm a Murphy. Bruce understands." I watched idly as sawdust covered the tip of my sneaker. Beads of sweat dotted his forehead and fell to the floor in slow motion.

"Damn arthritis is getting to me somethin awful." He cracked his knuckles.

"They're all tarred wid the same brush. Whew! I gotta take a wee break!"

He walked over to the door, looked out over the harbour and lit one of his rolled cigarettes. He threw the match outside on the gravel where it fizzled. I rested against the woodhorse, feeling the inner heat become part of me. He came back, bent and took my head in his calloused hands. His index finger was stained brownish-yellow with nicotine.

I flinched.

"Brown as a nut, ain't ya?" He moved my head back and forth, right then left. "Brown eyes like little chestnuts. Skin dark as a Jackytar. Hair almost black. Like yer mudder, ain't ya? Not much like us."

He chuckled, then grew serious again, his gaze steady. "I got somethin to ask ya, Alex. A favour. I wants ya to help yer fadder wid the chores. While Oi'm gone. Probably gonna be m'last trip out on the Bona Vister. Will ya?"

And little did he know, it had been his last trip. The ice was unforgiving, harsh and greedy. And soon his nemesis, my mother, would be buried beside him in St. Stephen's

Cemetery. But I kept my promise, even when we began to operate the bed and breakfast. When I wasn't studying, I was busy washing up the dishes, sweeping, doing load after load of laundry, ironing, painting inside and out when the weather was good, particularly those long stretches of fence. I actually enjoyed being outdoors painting, especially when sheep still roamed the hills of Bond Cove. The scenery was beautiful and it was gratifying to finish a project in the fresh air. And yes, I sawed up thousands upon thousands of sticks and then clove up splits for kindling, out in the ole store, as Poppy Murphy had done before me, and my father as a boy, too. Bruce never did pitch in much. Too busy playing hockey and being the school jock for that…

"Alex, watch out, b'y!" said Dad.

A dog lunged out of the ditch and yapped at the wheels. I swerved the car and narrowly avoided hitting it. Bruce scowled in the backseat. They were both wearing suits, while I wore dress pants and a sweater. Dad's was a respectable blue, with a crisply starched white shirt and a blue tie with red polka dots. I knew it was one of his Sunday suits. Bruce wore a much more hip black suit, with an expensive crème coloured shirt and a black silk tie. He appeared clean and well groomed, but there was no hiding the black circles under his eyes, nor the nervous twitch in his eyelid. I wondered again what demons plagued him. His hand slicked back a lock of wavy blonde hair from his forehead. The marriage band, of substantial gold, glittered, even in this dim light.

"Whatchu looking at?" he demanded.

Jackytar

Evelyn tut-tuted. She looked as new as a peeled egg. Glossy lips. Shiny hair. A smart black pantsuit with a gleaming white blouse collar.

"Nothing. Just looking, s'all," I said.

We turned into the paved parking lot of Barnes' Funeral Home. Several crows lit on the roof and power lines, squawked as if to greet us, then quieted down to watch. Horrid creatures.

Poppy Murphy used to say, "If a crow enters yer house, someone's gonna die."

Too late.

"Here we go," said Dad resignedly. We got out of the car and walked up the steps. Bruce sheepishly trailed behind. Evelyn was lecturing him about proper decorum.

Wouldn't hurt.

twenty five

■

A Misandrous Queer List

1. I cannot walk down the street holding hands with another male, even in the gay neighbourhood, without the threat of sneering remarks or violence from strangers.

2. I am not allowed to marry another male in many states, provinces and countries in the world; civil unions are not the same.

3. Literature for children rarely reflects my lifestyle by portraying same-sex partnerships. The characters are almost all white anyway.

4. Straight men are afraid to be alone with me because they may be perceived as gay, or fear that I might make a pass at them.

5. As a teacher, I am vulnerable to accusations of being a pedophile. Likewise as a father.

6. As a man, if I act "effeminate" or display so-called feminine traits such as caring, compassion and gentleness, I risk being punished. These are human traits.

7. I am expected to be competitive with members of my sex and only to confide in a female mate. Therefore, I am permitted few if any intimate friends of either sex.

8. When I report assault or abuse, whether sexual, physical, or verbal, there are few if any social services available to me, other than to treat me as a potential criminal. Especially if I am not white. And/Or from a low social class. And English isn't my native tongue.

9. I have a far greater chance of being imprisoned than any female. Especially if I am not white. And/Or from a low social class.

10. I have less chance of attending university than many women – at least many of the white, middle-class ones. Especially if I am not white. And/Or from a low social class.

11. Even though I am more likely to be the chief breadwinner in my family, I am often seen as an exploiter and privileged.

12. My health is not good. I am more likely to die of prostate cancer than a woman of breast cancer and have higher incidences of lung cancer, heart attacks and AIDS. Where is the public outcry?

13. My life expectancy is significantly lower than many females. Especially if I am not white. And/Or from a low social class.

14. When I die prematurely, my widow and offspring may benefit from my accumulated wealth and/or pension for many years. Only if I were a successful doctor, lawyer, or executive will I merit a big city newspaper eulogy with a picture.

15. I am more likely to be an alcoholic, drug addict, be in a car accident, commit suicide, or be homeless. Especially if I am not white. And/Or from a low social class.

16. If we divorce, I am unlikely to gain custody of my children, or even to get satisfactory visitation rights. However, a major chunk of my salary will still support them.

17. If I am a young unmarried father-to-be, there are virtually no services or parenting classes available for me, unlike for my pregnant girlfriend.

18. I have a far greater chance of being segregated in a remedial reading class or learning difficulties class. Especially if I am not white. And/Or from a low social class. And English isn't my native tongue.

19. Most of the role models I see of men in popular culture and media are brutish, selfish, aggressive, ignorant, foul, and/or idiotic.

20. I am rewarded for being a jock in school, but often treated with homophobia for anything else. Being bookish is considered gay.

21. My teachers are far more likely to consider me a discipline problem and to punish me. Especially if I am not white. And/Or from a low social class.

Jackytar

22. My teachers praise girls in my class more often and criticize them more gently.

23. In school, when I yearn for more active learning, including debate and movement, I am punished. Especially if I am not white. And/Or from a low social class. And English isn't my native tongue.

24. When I marry, I have only one respectable choice – work full-time. If I stray from full-time work, I am viewed as a parasite.

25. Although I work full-time, do repairs to the house, shovel snow, care for the vehicles, and drive the children around, unless I help with housework and food preparation, I may be called a chauvinist pig.

26. I have been taught and rewarded for being rough, insensitive and aggressive.

27. My worth in society is directly correlated to how rich and powerful I become. Should I lose this wealth and power, my spouse and social network will probably scatter like leaves.

28. I cannot cross my legs when I sit, talk with my hands, or wear tight clothes.

29. I can never truly attain manhood. It is impossible. This undying stress is with me every moment of every day.

30. When I die, no one will ever have truly known me.

twenty
six

∎

Had they filled them with cotton?

Dying, she'd reminded me of the many men I saw in Toronto, the fat eaten away from their faces and buttocks, too, by aggressive HIV medications. As many as 20 percent of the gay men in Toronto were rumoured to have the virus and many were taking medications whose side effects were sometimes as harsh as the symptoms of their various diseases. Maman's cheeks were suddenly plump and rosy. Mr. Barnes must have stuffed cotton in there and painted them with make-up. Her salt and pepper hair had been done as nicely as possible, too. Although sparse and dry, at least it looked clean, and was combed back behind her ears. Her eyes were, of course, closed.

She looked positively peaceful. An adjective that had rarely been used to describe her in life now fit in death. The coffin was a polished pine with brass handles and the inside red satin. Very refined. She wore her best church dress, a flowery dark blue linen dress. I was pleased to remark that her precious gold locket with the cherub inside would accompany her to the grave.

Then a moment of repulsion crept up on me. What was this custom of propping the dead up in coffins for public viewing, all gussied up?

I made a mental note to warn Keith to have me cremated, if ever anything happened.

"Hello, I'm Heather. Nice to meet you."

Rev. Byrne extended her chubby hand towards me. I tried not to show how startled I was by her obesity. The term, "tub of lard," sprung to mind. She was exactly as described, only fatter. Her fondness for deep fried chicken had evidently not been exaggerated. Her black cassock, ample and flowing on most clerics, was tight. Her armpits looked like there were basketballs under them, so extended they were from her body. The arms were supposed to be tight in such a gown, but the ample gown itself, falling to her ankles, should not have been.

"I'm Alex, as you know I'm sure. A pleasure to meet you. I've heard a lot about you. All good."

"Glad to hear that! That means I'm one step ahead, I guess."

She was tall, too, almost six feet and wearing black sneakers as much for comfort as to minimise her height, I imagined.

"I just wanted to tell you how sorry I am about your mother. She was truly a gift to the church these past years. I don't know what we'll do without her."

"That's what they tell me. You know Rev. Byrne, the mother I knew wasn't really much of a joiner. She was quite the loner all her life. I'm surprised to learn about this big change. I mean I'm glad to hear it, but puzzled. We weren't exactly close. Any ideas what the catalyst was?"

She spoke cautiously. "Well, life is strange, isn't it? I went to see France shortly after I started here. We needed a new organist. Aunt Flo had gotten older and was having difficulty keeping up. Her eyesight was worsening and her arthritis bothered her quite a bit. She was reluctant, but we finally convinced her to retire, poor ole dear."

"So Maman volunteered?"

I wondered what had transpired between them. I could almost picture Maman opening the door a crack, her brown eyes widening in surprise. She would have patted down her hair and smoothed over her top and slacks. Her top might have been stained from the incessant tea she drank and always managed to spill over herself and she would have been embarrassed. She was usually oblivious to such things, for she never saw anyone, so they didn't matter to her. She'd have been awkward, hesitant. Had she had the presence of mind to invite her in for tea or coffee?

"It wasn't that bad, you know," she responded, as if reading my mind. "She was quite happy when I told her about the position." Her eyes darted over my face. My disbelief must have been apparent, for she proceeded to qualify her statement with another low laugh. "I mean, she took some convincing, but she came around. Poor France. She was a pleasure to work with, Alex, a real pleasure."

Rev. Byrne's eyes wavered across the room. Evelyn was motioning for her to come over. She smiled at me apologetically.

"Alex, I better go talk to your sister-in-law. It was lovely meeting you."

I decided to push a little more. "One other thing, Rev. Byrne. Did Maman ever mention a tape of some sort

*J*ackytar

that she might have made?"

Her eyes widened and she stuttered. "A…a tape?"

"Yes, before Maman died, she spoke to me about a tape she'd made and not to let Dad have it. Does that ring a bell?"

"I don't know anything about that." She hesitated. "I'm playing one of her organ recordings at the funeral, but there's no reason she'd not want your father or anyone else to hear it."

"I see."

She was lying.

Evelyn had crossed over by this time and stood between us. I turned to the window. The sea had calmed and cold mist, what the locals called barber, was roving in. Rev. Byrne was hiding something, I was certain.

But what?

I looked around at the gathering, these people from my past, all familiar and well-wishing and yet somehow I felt antagonized. My partner, Keith, was conspicuously absent.

How would they deal if he were here?

Would they be polite?

Would they even understand that we were like a married couple?

There would be whisperings behind our backs, if not outright rudeness.

A solitary dory chugged across the harbour, returning to shore, the barber chasing it. Its passengers seemed to be a grandfather with his two young grandchildren. Bond Cove, and similar outport communities, had become relics from the past.

Who the hell became a fisherman these days? Work for a few months and draw unemployment for the rest of the year. It wasn't much of a life, but was mine any better?

We were caught between two worlds. Bond Cove – Newfoundland Theme Park, or go to the Mainland and experience "*dodo, métro, boulot.*"

I chuckled to myself, despite the hurt and uncertainty I felt.

"Hey, stranger! How ya doing?"

It was my former elementary school teacher. "Mrs. Kyle! How nice to see you. I'm fine. How are you?"

I could see that the day would be full of surprises.

Jackytar

t w e n t y
s e v e n

■

We sized each other up. Then hugged. She had matured into a grandmotherly figure; her hips wider, her always ample breasts ballooned. She'd stuffed herself into a tightish hand knit sweater. Her body was stout and yet she looked energetic, still capable of working long hours in her beloved garden.

"Just great, m'darlin."

"You look amazing," I said sincerely.

"Oh horse feathers and rubbish. Oi'm an old lady now." Her blue eyes glistened as she laid a compassionate hand on my arm. "Alex, Oi'm so sorry about your poor ole mudder, m'dear. My, she looks some lovely!"

She gestured towards the coffin.

"Well, at least she didn't suffer much, you know. It was quick. That's a blessing," I said.

"'Twas indeed. 'Twas indeed. Now how about I git ya a nice cuppa tay, eh? Come along wid me."

I followed her like an obedient pupil to the kitchenette

where I opted for coffee instead. She hasn't changed, firm yet kind, the sort of teacher who appealed to the gifted students and the down and outs. As for the mediocre who didn't push themselves, she had little time or patience.

"Coffee? That stuff'll kill ya, m'dear. Bad for the heart," she said. "Ya know, your mudder was such a godsend here at St. Stephen's. Always ready to lend a hand at our bakesales and eager to play at the services. Every Sunday, come rain or shine, she played, and weddings, christenings –"

She stopped herself in the nick of time from saying "funerals."

"He-yeah, she'll be sorely missed, that's for sure," she recovered.

Through the window, I spied St. Stephen's church, its steeple looming over the town. There were no buildings higher, other than the Pierce's homestead and Torbay House, perched as they were on opposite sides of a hill, vying for notice by the people of Bond Cove. Interesting that the Pierce side of the hill was called Spilling Hill and the other side Murphy's Hill. I knew every nook and cranny of that church, from the imported stained glass windows from Boston to the brass plaques for the young men who had sacrificed themselves during the Great Wars when we were still a British dominion.

I decided to prod her for more information regarding Maman's miraculous transformation, keeping the tone casual.

"But I thought Aunt Flo was the music director, Mrs. Kyle?"

She paused to nibble on a cookie. "Oh yis, m'dear, she was awright, but she got sick. So your mudder stepped in. He-yeah, she stepped up to the plate, she did, a real trooper. She told you how good she had it at the church, I spose?"

I had never thought of Maman as "a real trooper." Apparently, the tide had changed but no one had thought to inform me. When I'd called home, my questions about how everyone was doing were met with, "Grand" or "Awright, b'y, I spose." Then Dad or Maman would mention who'd gotten engaged, married, or had a baby. I'd hang up feeling invisible, left out of the loop and that's exactly how I felt now. Foolish as a caplin that I hadn't known about this change in Maman's life. Suspicious that they hadn't bothered to share it with me because I was gay and overlooked. I would have been pleased and excited for her.

I lied through my teeth. "Yeah, she mentioned that the church was taking a more active role in her life."

"Dear, what a treasure she was. I guess France started just after we got the new woman minister, Rev. Byrne." She pointed across the room to my sister-in-law and the minister engrossed in conversation. "You'd never know it, eh, that your mudder was the same woman. She came to life these past few years. Yup, we saw a side to France that we'd never witnessed before.

"She used to practise on the argan in the church almost every day, usually in the early marnings or evenings, when twas empty, ya know. Many a night Jane and I'd be out taking our constitutional and we'd hear her pounding away on the keyboards!" She chuckled. "She was very good, too." She leaned towards me conspiratorially. "Even better than Aunt Flo, but shhh! Don't tell a soul I said that! The recital she gave last summer was really something."

I gasped. "The recital?"

"Yis, didn't ya know? The recital she gave in August. Oh, m'dear, she played all sorts of composers. I think Bach was her main one. He-yeah, we must have had about farty or more people at the church. Twas really good. We all enjoyed it. Jane and I made about two hundred gingerbread cookies and four dozen lassy buns for the reception. Everyone said they were delicious."

"Oi'm telling ya, she really got people coming to the church she did, poor ole Francie! Everyone is saying how much they'll miss her. So creative. High strung like so many creative people are, but she was happy in the end. I wanted ya to know that, Alex, in case ya didn't. I knows ye all had your troubles wid her," she said compassionately, "but she came round in the end."

Mrs. Kyle took a tissue from her sweater and dabbed at her eyes. Although she'd mainly taught in primary and elementary grades, she'd been my teacher for a few courses in high school, too. I'd always been one of Mrs. Kyle's favourites. The teacher's pet. She admired my responsible attitude. If other kids were fooling around or inattentive, she knew she could count on me to remain polite and focussed and to influence them to get back on track.

I swallowed a lump in my throat. Maman had known some happiness after all, even if she had opted to exclude me from it. I tried to maintain a tone of casual interest.

"I'm glad to hear that, Mrs. Kyle. You've always been so good to us. Nice to know some things never change. How's Jane, by the way?"

"Oh she's grand. Right as rain. Same as always."

Ahh the secrets of Bond Cove. What was said and what

Jackytar

was never said. What was invisible and verboten. What everyone knew yet never confronted, or even dared to acknowledge. Some couples lived together until death. Some had affairs, like Poppy Murphy, and it wasn't deemed too scandalous if you were higher up on the social ladder. Or a woman with an abusive partner. Many couples changed partners or divorced. So what was it about the relationship between Mrs. Kyle and Jane that was so dangerous to name to the people of Bond Cove?

Was heterosexuality such a fragile thing?

Mrs. Kyle was actually Ms. Kyle. She'd never married, but no one ever dared call her anything other than Mrs. Kyle. As long as I had known her, she and Jane, as everyone called her companion, shared a house in the cove. Jane, a no-nonsense clerk at the Town Hall, was chatting with Dad by the coffin. Mrs. Kyle had to be a decade older than them, in her early seventies. I'd visited their house several times during my childhood, witnessed the affectionate pats, heard the inside jokes, saw the expressions they both immediately read on each other's faces, and intuitively understood; they were like so many other couples I knew. There was no doubt in my mind. Mrs. Kyle and Jane were lesbians, although perhaps they never used this term to describe themselves, despite having shared the same bed for forty years. Yet, no one ever acknowledged the lesbian nature of their relationship. Mind boggling. They were simply two spinsters fending for themselves as best they could without men or children. This earned them a certain respect about town and made them more available for volunteer work in the church and community, including babysitting.

Mrs. Kyle smiled. "And what are ya doing up there in

Toronto, anyways? France mentioned you were teaching?"

She asked this with considerable pride.

"Actually, I gave up teaching high school," I responded, "and shifted careers about three years ago. I teach at Ontario College, instructing teacher candidates and teaching French and English." I paused for courage. "I live with a friend. Keith. Together. He's in business. Works on Bay Street. We've been together for five years now. Five years already."

I stopped babbling.

I read puzzlement on her face, then recognition.

"I see, well, that's good, Alex, m'dear." Mrs. Kyle leaned towards me and whispered. "I always knew you'd do well. I always knew. Jane always said the same t'ing."

Her eyes crinkled. She patted my arm again, took her cup with her and headed towards her other half.

Déclic!

Even I play with words, I realized in the aftermath. Even I have difficulty telling the truth. Even I find the words hard to find, and harder still to utter. Even I am left dissatisfied by my blundering and the lies and the inadequacies of language. In this place of death, though, I was consoled by what just transpired between us.

She knew.

Jackytar

twenty
eight

∎

t w e n t y
n i n e

■

Dusk was phenomenal that evening. Tongues of red and orange licking at the harbour, marshes and forests. I felt unusually lonely, pensive, but waited to call Keith before he went to bed. We were an hour and a half later in Newfoundland, meaning I had to call him at 22h00 my time. He hadn't called last night, as promised.

"Sorry, I forgot," he said petulantly. Keith didn't like to be in the wrong. "I've been so busy with that new client I landed. I worked late last night and then fell right to sleep."

"I see," I answered. "And did you go out after work? Perhaps to Church Street, or was this straight boy's night out on Richmond?"

It had always annoyed me how my partner slid between his gay and straight life, as if he could neatly compartmentalize the two. To my knowledge, none of his work colleagues knew he was gay. He'd never invited me to any Christmas or end of year parties. I'd never met his boss. For all I knew, he had pictures of a phoney wife and kids in picture frames on his desk for all to see.

Straight decoys.

He inhaled sharply. "Naw, I didn't go out last night. Stayed home like I tole ya."

"Keith, is there someone there with you? I swear I can hear giggling in the background."

Silence…

"No one here but me. What's with the third degree, man? You're getting paranoid. So how's your mother, huh?"

I looked around my former bedroom, which Dad had converted into a comfy guest room once I'd left for Toronto. The queen-sized bed, covered by a burgundy comforter, was in the middle of the room propped against the beige wall. The wood trim along the ceiling was a deep mahogany and the dresser, too. A twenty inch television was centred on a stand adjacent to the window. The window was large and adorned with open velvet burgundy drapes, tied with a simple golden cord. There was no need to turn on the Tiffany-style chandelier, nor the matching lamp on the console table. Moonlight filtered in, bathing the room in silver. I looked at myself in the wing mirror of the dresser. Even in the shadows, the dark circles under my eyes were evident and the crow's feet seemed to etch themselves deeper and deeper every year.

I felt weary.

"She's gone, Keith. Passed away yesterday. We're in Bond Cove now. The wake was today. The funeral's tomorrow."

"Geez, I'm sorry Alex. Really I am. I dunno what to say."

"Are you flying down?"

Silence again. "Nope, sorry I can't. I really, really, really wish I could be there for ya. But I gotta get this new account cleaned up. And I'm flying to Vancouver day after tomorrow for a business meeting. Meeting investors from Seattle. The boss is nervous about this one. I absolutely gotta go."

Job's comforter. I traced the diamond pattern of the Mulberry rug with my toes. I didn't know why we played these games. Or why I couldn't seem to stop. "So ya can't be here, huh?"

"There's no way," he said rather abruptly, then recovered, "but I truly, truly am sorry for your loss." As if seeking my approval, he said, "I've been real good the last couple of days, Alex."

Perhaps to maintain the façade, too.

Paradoxes. Half-truths. Fictions we fabricated, then accepted as truth, and tried to pawn off to others. Fake and fragile, like so much of our knowledge. We both knew he was lying. I could hear him shushing someone and then a door closing. Some man he had picked up off the Internet probably, or at his favourite Church Street watering hole. Probably short and dark like me. His type. But younger. In better shape. A gym bunny.

Did this stranger even know Keith had a partner? Did he care?

I pictured them cavorting on the bedspread I'd picked out, drinking the wine I'd bought, using our lube and condoms. I imagined Keith cumming from this encounter with a stranger-lover and curiously, felt nothing.

"Listen, I'll check in with ya again tomorrow night, okay, sweetheart?" he said.

Curiously, being called *sweetheart* by another man never failed to cause a frisson of pleasure. Too bad I doubted that Keith really meant it.

Jackytar

"Alright. Bye."

Déclic!

Confronting death was only the beginning, I realized.

I remained pensive that entire evening and even paced; ghosts from the past did not lie still in Bond Cove. They quickened. They returned to prod my memories. To turn me into a little boy again. To make me remember who I was, where I came from, and what I wasn't and could never be. I was slowing awakening to the realization that I was Alex Murphy, the son of that French/Indian woman, grandson of the legendary Skipper Murph.

Tomorrow, I decided, I'd rifle through her things and if there really was a tape, I'd find it!

t h i r t y

■

Our creator who art in heaven,
Hallowed be thy name;
Thy kingd...dominion come;
Thy will be done on earth as it is in heaven.
Give us this day our daily bread;
And forgive us our debts,
As we forgive our debtors.
And lead us not into temptation, but deliver us from evil;
For thine is the ki...dominion,
And the power and the glory,
For ever. Amen.

thirty
one

■

Wednes*day*

DR Moose!
DR Moose!
DR Not
DR!
DR Deer!
Cedar Antlers?
DR Moose!

thirty
two

■

I devoured a Newfoundland breakfast. Bacon, eggs and thick slabs of white bread toasted over the woodstove spread lavishly with real, salty butter. Yesterday at the funeral home, Mrs. Kyle had gifted me with two lovely loaves of homemade bread. One of the loaves lay on the wooden cutting board, half eaten, crumbs scattered around the bread knife, its crust still glistening with butter. The kitchen was cluttered with food. In response to death, Bond Covians feed the living, I mused fleetingly, for reason had departed. This was a thing of the gut. Not a thing of the head. The fridge was crammed with tuna fish casseroles, meatloaves and plastic containers of fish n brews and Jiggs' dinner to slip in the microwave. I eyed the food hungrily.

Death had made me ravenous. I ripped the plastic wrap off a plate of lassy buns. They were dark brown from the molasses and brown sugar, packed with scrumptious bits of salt pork. I took a bite, slathered the gap left from my great maw with butter and stuffed a large morsel in my salivating mouth. I slopped strong coffee from the percolator into a mug and slurped it down. Next the gingerbread cookies with buttery icing. I was wolfing down yet another, feeling dreamy, when someone rapped at the door.

Who could it be?

My fingers were greasy with butter and bits of orangey gingerbread cookie, and suddenly I felt ashamed. Quickly, I rinsed my hands underneath the faucet and dried them on a dish rag. The knocking grew louder, more insistent.

I yelled: Coming!

In the hallway, I heard the incongruously slow ticking of the grandfather clock and hurriedly eyed myself in the mirror. I wiped crumbs from the corner of my mouth on my shirtsleeve and regained my composure. No longer the starved beast let loose in the kitchen.

I opened the door.

Recognition took a while.

He said: I'm very sorry, Alex. How are ya, stranger?

He grinned from ear to ear. I opened the door wide and stood back.

"I can't believe it's you! It's been years! C'mon in!"

I hung his overcoat up in the porch. He was wearing a black suit. He'd filled out since last I'd seen him. His physique had changed from that of a lanky young man to become much more muscular, but not bulky. Definitely not.

"I know. I heard about your mudder from Mom. So I decided to drive over from Harbour Grace for the funeral. I'm livin there now. With the parents."

"Please come in and sit down. Can I get you something

to drink? The coffee's fresh. Some tea, perhaps?"

"Tay'd be great."

The kettle was already boiled. I poured two cups. He still drank it with only sugar. I took milk and sugar in my own. His biceps bulged as he brought the tea to his mouth and swallowed. It registered that he was living with his parents and I was curious. But etiquette won out.

"You look the same," he said. "Haven't changed a bit."

"You're too kind. My hair's like a birch broom in the fits this morning. A bit greyer, too, than you probably remember."

I tried to sound light. I hoped my laugh lines weren't too visible and that he wouldn't notice the weight I'd put on.

"No, you look the same. Real good. In better shape even."

Was he blushing? Or was his face just wind burnt? If he had seen me gulping down that food a minute ago, I mused, he wouldn't say that.

"You look excellent, too. Still jogging?"

"He-yeah, jogging every morning, except Sundays. And I go to the gym four days a week, too. Lift weights. I'm addicted to exercise as much as ever. More. Keeps me sane."

He grinned. "That tay's some good! Warms the insides."

"There's lot's more. Would you like a toutin?"

He nodded, so I heated up a container of these fried dough cakes in the microwave and then placed them on the table next to the molasses.

"Thanks," he said, pouring on butter and molasses. "They're some good!"

Jackytar

"I think it was Mrs. Griffin who made them. Can't be sure. There's so much grub." I looked around the kitchen helplessly. "So what you been up to, AJ?"

He looked out the window, drawn to the Atlantic Ocean for answers and inspiration, as are all those of Newfoundland blood. "I dunno. Been lots of changes, I guess. You knew I became an engineer?" he asked rhetorically. "Well, I spose I was foolish as a caplin. That sure didn't work out."

He drank the tea gratefully and reached for another toutin. "May I?"

"Help yourself. There's food enough for an army here. You'd think there were ten more staying here, not one less."

He grinned again at my irreverent joke. "How'd she die?"

I repeated what Poppy Murphy used to say, "For want a breath."

He grinned again and waited, wolfing down the sticky toutin.

"She developed a malignant tumour. Inoperable. In the back of her head. She had a series of minute strokes and seizures. She'd been off for several weeks. But of course, it was difficult for anyone to notice at home. She stuck to herself so much. But her playing became affected at the church. Then she began stumbling and slurring her words. So they brought her to the Bond Cove Medical Clinic and from there we carted her to St. John's. She was admitted. Then she had a bigger stroke. The past week she was semi-conscious. Then she just died. Not too painful, I hope."

"She was young, though," he said. "How old was she?"

"Only sixty-three. How are your folks, by the way?"

"Dad's same as always. Loves goin fishin. Mom, she's excellent, b'y. Can't keep up wid her. She just retired from teaching. She enjoys being a nanny now to Sylvia's kid. Five years old. I'm an uncle."

"That must be nice."

I took a toutin and slathered it with butter and molasses. "Have a toutin or do wid'out un, eh?"

"Someone always says that!" He smiled at my feeble joke. "Alex, I loves that little child, I do. Adam's his name. Saucy as a crackie." He shook his leg to and fro underneath the table leg, a nervous habit he used to have when we were in student residence together. He looked at his watch. "Look, I don't wanna keep ya. The funeral's at two o'clock?"

"Yeah." We both got up and moved towards the door.

"I'll be there," he said in an intimate voice.

I handed him his grey overcoat and we shook hands. He looked more handsome than I remembered.

"Thank you, AJ."

He paused on the threshold. "Alexandre, it's nice to have you back. Can I come over? Maybe tomorrow? I'd like to talk."

There was urgency in his voice and trepidation.

"Of course. I'll see you at the funeral then."

He nodded and strode off towards his car, an unremarkable family car, unlike the sporty model he used to dream of one day owning. Dark green. The water was calm. Several crows screeched then flew off from the telephone line. He revved the engine as if it were a sports car and started out the driveway. He looked back at me and I at him.

Jackytar

Déclic!

Suspended time. Butterflies in my belly. Like I was on a roller coaster ride and had eaten too much cotton candy. A stearin darted down near my feet, stabbed some bug with its beak and then disappeared. I watched him drive down the long driveway of Murphy's Hill and along the shore until I could see him no more.

What was this ache in my heart?

thirty
three

■

A light, mysterious, joyful, mischievous
Travels fleetingly over your face
Dancing in your eyes
Flirting at the corners of your mouth
You laugh inside
We share a kiss that never was

thirty four

∎

We climbed the concrete stairs to the narthex and hung our overcoats on bronze three-pronged hooks. The church smelled similar to St. Matthew's Hospital. Of dust, old people, burnt candles, and decayed flowers. Fusty. They'd made efforts, these parishioners of Bond Cove, to spruce it up. The chipped stained glass windows of my youth were gone, replaced by newer, brighter, geometric panes that refracted the scarce sunbeams stubbornly piercing the fog. The new windows were brighter and clean cut, but lacked the panache of their ancestors. The revarnished pews smelled of lemon-scented polish. A banner guarded each side of the altar and they weren't dull purple things of aged velvet. No. The banner stage right was navy blue, with the words, "We are a community of love!" in huge white letters of cut cloth, the hippy symbol of peace, and white doves soaring towards the heavens. The banner to the left was even more startling, dozens of hands of different sizes and colours also cut from cloth, reaching upwards. Even in this small outport community, there was encouraging awareness of multiculturalism and diversity. The words, "We are one family," in light green cloth letters, adorned this hanging. The Anglican Church Women, I gathered, had been busy!

"Rev. Byrne'll be out soon," whispered father surreptitiously once we'd seated ourselves up front. "She's as wide as the devil's boots, that one."

"Dad!" I admonished, biting my lower lip in disapproval. "I already met her at the funeral home. She was nice."

People filtered in. Members of the Pierce and Johnson clans sat behind us. I recognized Geoffrey and Cynthia Pierce and Helen Clark, the librarian's daughter. She and I had gone to school together. Usually we sat behind them. Poppy Murphy had seen to our strategic seating with generous donations to St. Stephen's Church, so that his progeny would forever sit closer to God. Maman's coffin stood beside the altar, thankfully closed. I was relieved her gussied up corpse wouldn't be on display again, like a painting or sculpture in a museum to be gawked at. She was near her precious church organ for the final time.

How odd, this ritual of passage.

I knew I should feel grief and closure, but surprised myself by feeling puzzled and angry. Maman had had a new life these past years, but I'd been excluded. I would have preferred to have shared in her blossoming, but she hadn't let me in.

Rev. Heather Byrne came out of the vestry, her weight causing her to waddle and sway precariously, like a dory beyond the harbour in the hands of inept townies. She stopped at our pew. Her cheeks jiggled and she took Dad's

Jackytar

hand and spoke softly. "How are you all doing today?"

"We'll be alright, maid," replied Dad stoically.

"We'll start the service in a few minutes, then. It won't be long."

She patted him on the head. Death had transformed my father into a young lad again to be mollycoddled a bit. The service began once the last of the crowd had filed in, and a crowd it was. The church was full to the brim. The organ remained closed. A young girl I didn't recognize played solemn hymns on the piano, her fingers confidently flying over the keys. Her hair, yellow as beaten gold, glowed like an angel's halo in the subdued light and she held herself upright like a young regent.

"That's Morley's daughter's young maid," whispered Dad with pride. Morley was one of his oldest buddies. "She's some good at the piano! I was some glad when he told me she agreed to play today!"

The minister stood in front of the congregation, behind the altar. The choir, mostly older women, sang with enthusiasm but limited skill. They bordered on shrill, but I had to give them credit. They were doing their best. There were no men. Men rarely joined outport Newfoundland choirs. The odd skipper did sometimes roar through a hymn in his pew, oblivious to the harmonic discord, but thankfully none were present today. My predominantly gay church in Toronto had an amazing choir of men and women of various ethnicities and backgrounds, and gospel singers were sometimes invited, plus the whole congregation sang, and in harmony, too.

How strikingly different!

The rest was a blur, an overpowering sense of people surrounding us, the thick religious music swirling about our bodies, the smell of incense and burning candles, the coloured panes of red, green and blue incongruous in the solemn atmosphere, until her eulogy. She forced herself into the beautiful oaken pulpit, wearing it like a skirt. Then she folded her hands and something magical occurred.

She spoke and her voice was wisdom, compassion and intelligence, confident and crystal clear, carrying itself effortlessly throughout the church. It was the voice of an angel.

"Ya know, Jesus once said, 'I have come so that you may have abundant life' (John 15:7-11). I think this is one of the most poignant passages in the Bible, and it's certainly governed my life." She took off her glasses, then put them on her nose again, as if changing her mind, and looked out over her flock. "And many of ya have heard me say that in the past. I believe that both joy and suffering are okay. Yup, we can permit ourselves to grieve the loss of a loved one and yet be joyous for having loved that person. In this present moment today, we are here not only to lament the loss of our beloved sister, France Murphy, but also to celebrate her life."

She nodded toward the coffin. A coffin of polished pine with a red coloured satin pillow and lining, I knew. Brass handles. And the body of Maman.

"When I came here we were losing our devoted church organist, Aunt Flo, and I knew that Christmas was coming up, and weddings, and I had to prove myself! So I inquired and several people mentioned France Murphy. They cautioned me that she was the quiet, reserved type, except at Christmas, but this was early summer and I hadn't seen that side of her yet. Well, France's quiet nature was an understatement! She rarely ventured from her

Jackytar

home at that time and she had few, if any, friends. Her devoted husband. Her family. But other than that?

"Yup, when I first met France, I'd been told she was a little bit odd, and I mean no disrespect." She smiled at us, the family. Muffled titters filtered throughout the church, but they were not unkind. "I went up to that beautiful house. It even had a name. Torbay House. I knew one of the most community-involved families in Bond Cove lived there. The Murphys. And I knocked at the door."

She mimed knocking. "I felt like a nervous little girl selling cookies, knocking on a stranger's door. Then this wee little woman came to the door and peered out the crack. It was France. She hesitated. Then she seemed to make a decision and opened the door. I'm sure she was as afraid of me as I was of her. I told her who I was, but of course, I was wearing my collar, so I think she knew. She invited me in and, of course, we had a cup a tea!

"We talked that day for hours. Hours and hours. It was pitch black before I left. But I knew I had found a good soul, a kind soul, a gifted soul. Most of the day we spent in her sitting room. That beautiful room, small but laden with treasures, touches of her unique personality. It was her very own sanctuary and, I think, in some ways, her prison. Now let me explain. The shelves were lined with volumes and sheets of music, some quite rare. A lovely silver tea service adorned a beautiful Edwardian table that was polished like a mirror! I had never seen a real tea service before, a silver one. I'd read about them, but never seen one. She had one! And something special transpired that day.

"What did we discuss, you might ask. Why did this shy woman, some might even have referred to her as a recluse," Rev. Byrne looked around the church, "open up to me and even spill her soul? Was it my minister's collar?" There was gentle laughter again. "Was it my knowledge of biblical scripture?"

She paused for a few seconds.

"Well, no, it's because I spoke to her. I spoke to her and I listened. Too often we talk, but we don't listen. I'd heard that she knew the organ and I saw before me a woman who was in a shell.

"'I have come so that you may have abundant life,' said Jesus.

"So I went to her, because I wanted to see what France Murphy was about! And ya know what, I got to know her, you got to know her and we all got to know each other. This woman was a true gift to our congregation!"

Beside me, Dad dabbed at his eyes with his fingers. The box of tissues jammed in the pew rack remained untouched. He wasn't as unemotional as I had predicted and I was glad. Then he seemed to catch himself and looked guiltily downwards. More men should show emotion, I thought. If only Maman had also been more in touch with her emotions, and they'd been able to better confide in each other, things might have been different.

"That auspicious day, she played for me on that old pump organ in her music room. It took some coaxing first. And then she played. She played and played, and I listened. She lost herself in music. It was an antique pump organ, in perfect condition. She played lovely hymns. I remember I closed my eyes at one point and the beautiful melodies of Bach carried me to heaven…" Rev. Byrne closed her eyes for a moment as her voice trailed off and then she looked upwards, "and she played."

Jackytar

"'I have come so that you may have abundant life,' said Jesus.

"Ya know, joy and wisdom are found in our music, in our singing, in our dance, in our painting, in our yarning, yup, and in our worship. Fishing with pride is celebrating the joy of life and Christ. Knitting those cute little booties for a small grandchild is celebrating the joy of life and Christ. And playing the organ for others, not only alone with no one to hear, can also be celebrating the joy of life and Christ. I said to her, 'France, you need to share your gifts!'

"That Christmas Eve celebration turned out to be the highlight of the year and of my career. I'd never felt so much love and caring and joy in a church before and it was largely due to the beautiful music that filtered through our church and into our hearts. France played and we sang. We sang and we praised and we celebrated having each other and God.

"'I have come so that you may have abundant life,' said Jesus.

"I firmly believe that we should celebrate our accomplishments as individuals and as a church. We should celebrate our differences, too. France brought us the understanding that we all have gifts that are hidden away, just aching to come out! We all have reasons to come out and share our joy together, but sometimes we aren't encouraged to. Sometimes we need a little help, a little support, a little push. Someone to listen and someone to appreciate.

"Now I know France's family was wonderful to her, but sometimes we need to go beyond the family to a larger community. That day, and in later conversations, for France and I grew to become friends, I learned a lot about this courageous woman.

"She grew up on the French Port-au-Port peninsula, *la péninsule de Port-au-Port*. She told me they were poor. Her mother had several children and their father died when she was young. She always lamented her lack of formal education.

"They spoke French at home. The one saving grace, the one thing she cherished most, was the pump organ her mother had gotten her. Now I have a story to tell you. They were poor. Poor and French speaking. No father in the family and just getting by. Sometimes, she told me, it was a struggle just to put a proper meal on the table and sometimes they went without. Yet, her mother took the children to church every single Saturday. They were French and Roman Catholic, although as ya know, France later converted to Anglicanism when she and Julian married in St. John's.

"Yup, her mother always loved church music and even managed to sing in the choir at their church and had her children join the junior choir when they were old enough. Then France sang in the senior choir. Although they had no money, they took any work they could get. Her mother cleaned homes and France helped as soon as she was able, caring for her three younger brothers and then, when she was older, working alongside her mother doing laundry for others, cleaning homes and babysitting. She officially gave up school after grade six to help her family.

"There was a lady organist at their church, a Mme Lafitte, France told me. And when she spoke about this woman, she glowed. Mme Lafitte was in better circum-

Jackytar

stances. Mme Lafitte's husband was mayor and she gave music lessons to the families in the area who could afford it. Now this woman was not rich herself, but they were comfortable.

"One day, France's mother let it slip how she wanted her daughter to learn music. Mme Lafitte didn't hesitate. She offered her free lessons. From that day onward, France had discovered a new meaning in life, away from the cleaning and child rearing. She discovered music and her love of the organ grew and grew. She couldn't go to school anymore, but she always had her music lessons and she went at least twice a week from age eight onward.

"She told me she used to skip to this woman's house, about a mile away. She'd finish her washing, her ironing, her bed making, and diaper changing, and she'd skip to her lesson, no matter how tired she felt. She said to me, 'Heather, the *musique* was a light to me. It filled me wid light.'

"'I have come so that you may have abundant life,' said Jesus.

"So you had this little girl, French-speaking, poor, who had quit school to help her overworked mom. And she loved music. She loved her music lessons. And it was all due to a slipped comment by her mom and the openhearted generosity of a stranger. She and her mother even managed to scrape together enough money to buy her the second-hand organ she kept all of her adult life.

"It wasn't until she turned sixteen and left for the big city to get work, that she really learned English. But she always kept that French accent. She went to work for a wealthy St. John's family as a maid. They were kind to her, she said, and the bit of extra money she was able to save

DOUGLAS GOSSE

159

after sending most home to her family, went in organ lessons with a new teacher.

"But France kept her shyness. She had her troubles and she began to retreat more and more into herself. Ya know, Julian and I discussed this eulogy and we agreed we would be honest. France suffered through some really bad times. But we can all agree the last few years were music to France and to us.

"We came to appreciate and love this woman, France, who, until sickness claimed her just a few short weeks ago, had opened up and shared her music with us. She opened up, and although her voice was a soft one, her music was loud and powerful and spiritual and healing.

"'I have come so that you may have abundant life.'

"We saw France not only play at services, at Christmas and Easter, at weddings and yes, at funerals. But also she directed the junior and senior choirs, and she was always available to help in food drives, in collecting clothing for the poor and in raising money for cancer research."

She stopped and looked sideways in contemplation. Then she waved her right index finger in the air as inspiration hit her.

"For some, we name a vision of how we want the world to be. For others, our contribution is as part of a team, or in helping others, or in giving financial resources. France did all of these. There is leadership and there is followership. Leaders rely on followers, on their support and commitment. Both need each other. France became a leader, someone we could count on, someone whom we all loved."

Sniffles around the church. Rev. Byrne turned and walked out of the pulpit. She stood beside Maman's coffin.

Jackytar

"My friend had a horse. A fine horse until it started to limp. Now I don't know if you know much about horses, but when they limp, they're often put down. So he brought it to a vet and the vet removed a small pebble from its hoof." She reached into a pocket of her cassock and held up a round pebble for all to see. "The horse walked fine afterwards. It limped because of this small pebble!"

Rev. Byrne was a gifted exegetist, much like my pastor in Toronto. And like him, it was evident that she was genuine, that she cared deeply and had conviction.

I sensed someone staring at my back and glanced behind me. People were listening with rapt attention. AJ was there amidst the crowd and we made brief eye contact. His presence comforted me.

"Sometimes, I think, in our own lives, we're stopped by small obstacles. Not that France's hardships weren't real. They were. Yup, being a woman, being French in environments where English was mostly spoken, being poor and having low self-esteem, were as real as real can be. Her circumstances created the little girl she was and the woman she was to become. But then she came alive. She came alive again. Fifty years later, that little girl skipping to her organ lessons became a middle-aged woman skipping to her beloved organ here at St. Stephen's."

She smiled benignly, lifted her hands towards the heavens and peered upwards. Her voice was thoughtful and low, but none had difficulty hearing, I was sure.

"'I have come so that you may have abundant life,' said Jesus.

"France opened up her heart and her soul and she gave. She gave and she gave, and we love her for it. We will always love her for it, for we're so much the better for having shared in her life.

"Now the hard part."

Rev. Byrne reached into her pocket and held up a cassette for all to see.

"I have here a tape that France made last year," she choked, "on which she recorded some of her favourite hymns and I'd like us to play her all time favourite now for you to hear and remember. Let the music surround you. Immerse yourselves in its beauty and remember our dear mother, wife and sister, France Murphy.

"'I have come so that you may have abundant life.'

Bruce remained poker faced.

I wept.

Jackytar

thirty
five

■

Our F…creator who art in heaven,
Hallowed be thy name;
Thy…dominion come;
Thy will be done on earth as it is in heaven.
Give us this day our daily bread;
And forgive us our debts,
As we forgive our debtors.
And lead us not into temptation, but deliver us from evil;
For thine is the king…dominion,
And the power and the glory,
For ever. Amen.

thirty
six

■

Thursday

The day after the funeral, I went to the shop to pick up some items: shampoo, shaving gel, lip balm. Really an excuse to get out and move around. There were teenagers on the stoop of the shop. Wearing jeans and bulky jackets. Silence as I approached. They stared. Five of them.

Good morning: I said.

Silence.

I spent a few minutes looking around the shop.

The storekeeper was a woman in her thirties, big-breasted, vibrant red hair, a nice smile. Sharon. We chatted for a few minutes. She was pleasant. She put my items in a plastic bag. And I started to leave.

G'bye: I said at the door.

I spoke to the seated teenagers: Excuse me.

They barely budged. I weaved through them, awkward-ly. I walked away, their eyes burning a hole in my back.

One muttered under his breathe: Gay.

Another coughed: Pansy!

Faggot!

Louder this time. Bolder.

What a trick, to cough and say pansy at the same time, I thought. They laughed, these teenagers on the stoop of the shop, shrill mocking laughter and dismissive deep guffaws. These teenagers with nowhere to go. In expensive blue jeans and bulky jackets. Haircuts and attitudes copied from television sitcoms and music videos. I wondered who their parents were, their guardians. Who took care of them, taught them? Who nourished their minds, souls and intellects? I could've had one this age. Still want one. To love and cherish, to help grow and learn in this world. To show the richness and wonder of life and diversity to.

Quelle honte!

I turned around.

It stopped.

What are you gawking at?

Pansy. From the French word *pensée*. Come to mean *pensive* in English. Thoughtful. Gay, a word denoting and connoting pride or derision. Depending on who uses it and the context. Are pensive males seen as gay, then, and punished for it?

Faggot. From the Inquisition. When faggots, or sticks, kindling, were used to burn gays at the stake. Alive. Like witches. Contemporary use meant to insult, injure, belittle, humiliate, emasculate, de-male.

They seemed embarrassed. Stared at the ground. I shrugged and walked away. Towards home. My heart racing. I looked over the water. The stearins and gulls swooped down around the Government Wharf with alacrity.

Day after day.

The ocean was choppy. The wind cold on my face.

My cheeks burned.

DOUGLAS GOSSE

thirty
seven

■

That afternoon, I walked down Harbour Road, past the saltbox houses of red, green, beige, yellow, and white. Past the landwash where I'd collected driftwood to earn a badge as a boy and used to look at spiders and dead things the Atlantic Ocean had tossed ashore. I smelled kelp and rotting seaweed. I smelled the wood of sun dried and rotting driftwood and of neglected fences belonging to those increasingly deserted houses. I walked past Ole Man Howell's bungalow. His missus had died just a few months ago, I recalled. Women usually outlived men in Newfoundland, too. Men drank and smoked more and broke their backs fishing, hunting, driving trucks, cutting wood, and building houses; they worked twelve hour shifts, too, whether in rural Newfoundland or on Bay Street. Fishermen, loggers, truckers, construction men, academics, brokers, bankers, lawyers, and executives. Didn't matter.

Once Keith had been drunk on wine and unusually chatty. It was his birthday, the first we'd shared together. He'd graduated from an elite private secondary school for boys in Toronto. He called himself an Old Boy. He'd explained to me the unwritten codes: never permit yourself to appear vulnerable, especially not in public; fight to be successful, to win at any cost; get a beautiful girlfriend and excel at sports.

Fit in or die.

Keith slurred that his private school had trained him well for the rigours of Bay Street. He'd downed his glass of wine and half joked that men were clones in his alma mater and now at work. Even their clothes were identical. Their haircuts. Their cars and memberships. Their wives blonde and slim with perfect smiles and wardrobes, professionally educated usually, but devoted to charity work and propping up their husbands through the executive wife network. Everyone falsely gracious and just waiting for a fault or weakness to manifest so they could pounce.

Also in faraway Bond Cove, expressing emotion other than bravado and aggression – mythical male qualities that supposedly kept you on top – was fiercely regulated.

But at what price, I wondered?

There was a thing called soul.

I walked past the last wharf. Men could cry when there was no question of their masculinity being in doubt, on a battlefield, or in national hockey if you were a big enough star. But not at funerals, not even at the loss of a wife or mother. It was a matter of pride, this being a man. I paused and stared at the ocean.

Déclic!

Although it was never spoken, everyone knew that you could never arrive at manhood, and even if you had for a moment, you could never keep it. It had to be constantly earned, reinforced, regulated, suffered, and embraced. And yet it had to be portrayed as completely natural, normal, effortless even.

What hypocrisy!

Everyone knew, or suspected on some level, how truly fragile it was, this shaky manhood. Thus, the frenetic regulation, the panicked and desperate affirmations of being a so-called man. And the quotas of men in jail, dead before their time, or living like zombies on the streets of cities and even smaller towns. The alarming numbers of boys failing in school and the dwindling numbers of males in universities and trade schools. All solemnly reminded us that society was shifting and maleness as we knew it might be better off discarded in the landwash.

Was being discarded in the landwash.

I strode past houses where townies now dwelt. They had bought them at a steal for use as cottages during weekends and vacations. Bond Cove was fast becoming a ghost town, had been since the seventies. Many homes were already deserted. Had been for years. Boarded up. Falling into disrepair. The grass in the front gardens overgrown and needing to be made into hay. They would be appalled, these proud, dead Newfoundlanders, so hard-working and mindful of their property. Poppy Murphy would have made short work of the grass in his day. His trusty sickle so razor sharp that if you tested your finger on the blade, it'd bleed like crazy. Of course, he could test his own finger on the curved blade. The palms

Jackytar

of his hands were as tough as snarbuckle. Like an animal, he'd adjusted to his environment and role in life.

Through thick and thin.

I walked onto Brigg's Road, in obvious disuse, sprinkled now with pebbles and rocks, the bumps and holes much worse than I remembered. The Town Council had their hands full. I stopped at Johnson General Store. Utterly dilapidated. I remembered the enduring smell of molasses, flour and salted fish from the barrels that were kept for decoration when I was a boy. And the wooden shelves lined with jars of jam and tins of beans, vegetables and fruit. And the coloured boxes of tea with their elegant swirls. And the glass counters filled with bags of candied popcorn and big glass jars of multicoloured hard candies. Poppy Murphy used to buy black licorice for isself and peppermint knobs for Bruce and me. The old metal scale hanging from the ceiling, its hook swaying and sometimes creaking, used to fascinate me. The mannequins frightened me and yet I was drawn to them. They looked so real and yet they weren't; their faces painted, skin an unnatural beige, lips too red. Like drag queens, really, although I wouldn't have made that analogy at the time. They scared me. They were and yet they weren't.

"What'd wrong, m'son?" Poppy'd ask.

"Nutten t'all."

Never fear. Never admit weakness. Never show emotion.

I left it all behind when I moved to Toronto.

And now I was back.

I trod past the houses, down the winding road, to Shepherd's Bluff. How I still loved these cliffs, the freezing wind and the cobalt ocean. Irish pirates had buried treasure there beneath the ground long ago. More than one had attempted to find it with metal detectors over the years, but no go. I wove my way down the mossy footpath. The drang was well worn, but the sheep and goats were no longer. Rocks and pebbles collided and rolled to the bottom. But I was used to the steepness. Like a stubborn Billy goat, I had climbed up and down this same drang hundreds, no thousands of times. I could do it with my eyes closed.

At the bottom, I sat on My Rock, arms outstretched on the armrests. I looked at the old scar on my wrist, faded now, of course, but the small, thin line still visible to me. I faced the Atlantic Ocean and I wailed. Not weeping. Not crying. But a deep down feral howling as the ocean spray and wind whipped around me, mingling with the pain, disguising my hurt.

For her.

For the children.

For myself.

For all who lived the hatred I couldn't escape, no matter where I went. Even on this remote island. Among my own people.

Home.

Jackytar

thirty
eight

∎

When I returned to Torbay House, Evelyn was welcoming visitors into the front parlour for tea like a nineteenth century countess in her Parisian salon. I popped in to say hello. She'd baked last night and early this morning. Several dozen buns. Ginger cookies, light on the ginger. Couldn't be too spicy. And she'd taken down bottles of preserves from the pantry. Strawberry and partridgeberry jams and my favourite, bakeapple jam, worth its weight in gold even though my Mainlander friends tended to dislike the tiny seeds. Evelyn had a glow not unlike a bride. Although outwardly she tried to project solemnity, nobody was fooled. Her excitement was palpable. She was overjoyed to be host and centre of attention.

I crept upstairs into Maman's room and sure enough, the key to her music room still hung on a hook inside her walk-in closet. Her clothes were mostly nondescript, bought in department stores, except for a few brighter, more stylish dresses on the right. She had been turning over a new leaf, these clothes confirmed. Pity, now it'd have to all go to charity, unless Evelyn wanted a few items, which I doubted. Evelyn was taller and more full-figured, with muscles from countless hours of aerobics and working out at the neighbourhood gym in St. John's. These clothes, even the more stylish ones, were too small and cheap for her urbane taste.

I listened at the top of the stairs, but heard only muffled voices from the front parlour. If Bruce was around, he was either entertaining guests with his wife or taking a nap somewhere. I tiptoed down the stairs and turned the key in the lock, holding the Christmas wreath to be as noiseless as possible. The grandfather clock in the hallway chimed on the hour and my heart leapt into my throat. I entered swiftly and closed the door quietly behind me.

Ah, that scent! Maman's scent, a faint lilac perfume, lingered in the room. It was as Rev. Byrne had described, her sanctuary. As usual, images of her precious cupid, seraphim and cherubs filled the room. Yet, whereas she'd always kept the music room clean and fresh, the room now displayed a joy of spirit as never before! The planching was similar to the hallway, but with a more reddish tinge. The beige walls had a hint of ochre. The *oeil de bœuf* window frame glistened with bright varnish and a pretty lace doily adorned the steamer trunk. Her music books stood at attention on the shelves, but she had interspersed photos and angel figurines between volumes and on the Edwardian table where her silver tea service gleamed. There were recent photos of the church, Rev. Byrne and the choir. She even had wedding photos of Bruce and Evelyn and Christmas pictures of Bruce and me as children. My graduation picture for my master's of

Jackytar

education degree was the sole item on the end table.

Figuratively, she had let me into her sacred abode to share in her life!

One thing struck me as odd. Other than some garland haphazardly draped over the shelves and a plastic mask of the *Père Noël* pinned to the bathroom door, the room was devoid of Christmas decorations. Usually by early November, she'd already have extensively decorated her music room into a Christmas fantasy. Her illness, no doubt.

I poked around but found no tapes. Her pump organ sat there, forlornly, waiting for its musician, the seat a bit haphazardly out of place. My eyes settled on the steamer trunk. The elegant doily was slightly askew and garland lay furled up next to it in the corner. Behind the doily were several of her little cherub dolls in a clutter. I lay them on the Edwardian table. I folded the doily and lay it on the overstuffed armchair, which she'd upholstered in a smart floral print to match the walls. The trunk was locked. I lifted the lid of the pump organ.

Thank God! The key was still in its hiding place on a small protruding ridge.

Inside, the trunk was a tad messy by Maman's standard, too. I wondered if anyone else had been poking around in there. Then I reasoned: perhaps with her illness, she hadn't been able to maintain the same level of neatness. Her music books were organized in transparent folders that she must have ordered from St. John's, or picked up during a visit to Bruce and Evelyn. She loved that little rustic music shop down on Water Street that had catered to the eclectic tastes of its refined clientele since the mid-eighteen hundreds. Then I saw it.

On the right side was a black leather case and alongside it a palm-sized tape recorder, expensive and state of the art. I lifted out the case and opened it. Inside were neat rows of tapes, all dated, titled and numbered. I took out the first level from the leather tape case and examined the tapes more closely. Bach. Mozart. Solo pieces. Some were recordings of her own playing, all chronologically numbered at fairly regular intervals from the past few years, corresponding to the time when Rev. Byrne had visited and Maman had taken a new lungful of the air of life.

The last tape case was empty.

It was dated two months ago, but unlike the others, it was labelled with her maiden name, France Gabriel, and titled *Témoignage* or *witnessing* in English. Could this missing tape be the key, the one she'd cautioned me about on her deathbed, that she didn't want Dad to hear? Was *Témoignage* more than just the name of music she'd composed and played? Was it some sort of personal diary or testimonial?

What had she hidden, what truths had she kept to herself until she could no more and felt compelled to record them? All other tapes were present. I searched in her special music room and then in her bedroom.

No nook or cranny was left uncovered but still no sign of the missing tape.

Where could it have gone?

Jackytar

thirty
nine

∎

Soldiers found this message written in the cellar of a Polish farm after World War II. The person − man, woman, or child − we don't know, had scribbled on the rock wall with chalk:

"I believe in the sun when it's not shining, and in God, even when he's not talking to me. I believe in love, even when it's not shown…"

— Rev. Dr. Brent Hawkes

f o r t y

■

That evening, I was discretely looking around the house for the cassette when I heard a knock at the door. My old friend, with whom I'd shared my dreams as a youth, or at least most of my dreams, stood there grinning like the AJ of old.

"Is this a bad time?" he asked.

"No, not a'tol, AJ. Good to see you. C'mon in."

We settled in the kitchen again and I served tea and lassy buns.

"Hmmm. Very tasty! Delicious!"

"I'd like to take the credit but Evelyn made them for her guests today. My speciality's date squares."

"No way? Jaysus, I haven't had any date squares in a dog's age. I'd kill for some right now."

"How bout we make some, then?"

"Are you kidding? Yeah! Let's do it!"

He rolled up the sleeves of his shirt. I looked in the cupboard for Dad's recipe books. Even though I probably knew the recipe by heart, I wanted to be sure and follow his recipe to the letter. My time was drawing short in Bond Cove, Newfoundland, and if authenticity meant taking the time to double-check a recipe, so be it. Also, his date squares had always reminded me of Poppy Murphy's, whose own were unparalleled. Regrettably, Poppy Murphy had carried his recipe, or his knack for making them, to the grave.

<u>Newfoundland Date Squares</u>
1 $^{1/2}$ cups flour
1/2 teaspoon salt
1/2 teaspoon baking soda
1 $^{1/2}$ cups quick rolled oats
1 cup brown sugar
1 package dates
1/2 cup butter
1 cup hot water

"Whattaya doing now, Alex? Still teaching?"

We rummaged around for the ingredients and set them on the table.

"I taught for several years in St. John's, then in Toronto. Then I parlayed into teacher pre-service programs. I instruct teacher candidates in a Bachelor of Education program at Ontario College." We started cooking the dates, brown sugar and hot water. "I'm cross-appointed. I also teach in the English and French, second language programs. Lots of adult learners from Asia and Europe. I like it a lot."

"Sounds like you lucked out. Like you really enjoy your job."

DOUGLAS GOSSE

I refilled the cups with more tea from the teapot and stirred the saucepan. "Did you know that cleaning the inside of a teapot is wrong, even when it's tarnished?"

The mixture turned soft and he set it aside to cool.

"Of course. Everyone knows that," said AJ.

His eyes roamed over the spread of food littering the counters and tabletop. Laughing with him came as easily as riding a bike after years of abstinence, or swimming again. Natural and unforced. Like putting on an old favourite sweater that fit just so. Like my turtleneck sweater, seventeen-years old, my oldest item of clothing by far and the most cherished.

"So engineering wasn't your cup of tea, eh?" I asked. "I kind of suspected as much."

"Nope, not a'tol. How'd you know?"

"Well, you always struck me as someone who was more interested in the social sciences. I could never figure out why you'd didn't go into something you were more interested in."

He looked at me thoughtfully.

"Well, first of all, my parents always encouraged me to be an engineer when I was growing up and so did my teachers. Dad was a mechanic. Thought I could do better. Git into a profession. Mom was a nurse. Said the sciences were where it was at. Told me I'd have job security. And when you're a student, they have people come in to visit the faculty. They tell you how much you're gonna be making. Starting at $50,000 to $60,000! Not bad, eh, for a young fella from around the bay? Then you do your co-op placements and you slowly realize that something isn't right. There just aren't that many positions for chemical engineers. It was all a lie."

Jackytar

AJ sifted the flour, baking soda and salt into a mixing bowl. I added oats and brown sugar. He mixed it up vigorously with a wooden spoon.

"I applied to all the ile companies off shore and didn't even git an interview. Most of those jobs went to fellas from Norway and the Mainland. Everyone told me to do engineering and I'd be set for life. What a joke! My uncle Dave, Mom's older brudder, died aboard the Ocean Ranger, but still they told me that was where the money and security was. So in high school, I took all the sciences and math courses I could. Physics and chemistry. Advanced calculus. Worked like a dog. Engineering was what they all told me to go for. So I did."

AJ added butter. When all was blended, I pressed half of the crumbs into a well-greased 8 x 11 inch pan.

"He-yeah," I said.

"When I graduated from university, my parents gave me a brand new stereo system as a gift. They were so proud. They thought I was set. That my future was laid out for me. That I wouldn't have a hitch.

"I got my first job for a company in Corner Brook. I set up a chemical laboratory. Tested ile samples. I had a decent apartment. Bought a second-hand sports car but she was a nice vehicle. Only sixty thousand clicks. I wore my engineering ring everywhere I went. The money wasn't bad, not great, but not bad. They told me there'd be increases in six months to a year and then we'd talk about health and pension plans. So I completed a kind of probationary period. I didn't complain and did it all. Worked my ass off. Contacted the contractors by myself. Made the orders. Processed all the paper work. Took me about six months. Everything was runnin like clockwork.

I put in at least ten hours a day and extra time on weekends, even though there was no overtime pay. This was what I had worked for. I was makin it."

AJ covered the pan with date filling and topped it up with the remaining crumbs.

"Then they fired me. Right out of the blue. Just like that! I had kind of figured as much. In meetings before they fired me, they talked about gettin a co-op student to do some of the paper work and administrative detail that I was doing, but I never imagined they'd fire me. I didn't put two and two together. Which is ironic after all those math courses.

"But I guess they knew he'd do it for ten dollars an hour. Then when he got sick of it, they could easily git another one. They had no qualms. No remorse. All they cared about was the bottom line. Typical capitalist bullshit."

"So what'd you do?"

"I moved back to town. I applied everywhere and couldn't git a single job in my field. I was so depressed, I spent the summer crying in my beer. Goin downtown almost every night. Fartin around. A man's worth is based on his job and how much he earns, right? And I was tapped. I had none. I was drawin unemployment. I thought there'd be more opportunities in St. John's, or at least better access to resources, employment agencies, networking. Good luck! I felt like a big loser.

"Finally, it was August. I woke up one day with the biggest friggin hangover! I was livin with three other guys in a house on Long's Hill. It was a dump and they were slobs. I remember goin out to the living room and there were beer bottles all over the place and ashtrays overflowing. I cleared a spot off the couch and lit my last cigarette.

Jackytar

"I remember looking at the flame and thinkin about my life. I remember lookin out the window and seein the water. Then I thought of you."

"What do you mean?" I asked.

"What you used to say about having a life that matters. Remember? A life that counts. A life that we can look back on with pride. That day was the end of that chapter in my life. I moved out of that dump the next day."

"Wow. I didn't know I'd been that much of an influence."

"Well, you were. I drove home to Harbour Grace. Mom and Dad let me move back home wid em. I ended up stayin around the bay for a term. My parents didn't know what to make a me. We had a few rows but it all worked out. I never touched a single drop of booze or another cigarette. I started jogging every day, like we used to. Remember that?"

Déclic!

I nodded. How I used to love jogging on Rennies Mill path and around Quidi Vidi Lake, the two of us barely taking the time to warm up, cocky in our youth, then panting for a few minutes until we gained a rhythm. The silence. No talking. Just a rhythmic pounding on the ground and a sense of connection to the environment and to each other. From time to time, one of us would sprint and the other would give chase, giggling and playing a carefree game of tag until we collapsed on the grass with uncontrollable laughter. Then we'd share our philosophies and observations of life, looking up at the sky.

Those were some of the happiest moments of my life.

But all I said was, "Yeah, I remember, AJ."

"Well, I filled out an application for a criminology course and sent it off. So I sold the car, which wasn't hard. She was a good car. I moved back to St. John's and got an apartment after Christmas. A two-year college program and I loved it. Not even university, but college. Nothing to do with engineering whatsoever and I was happier than I'd ever been before. Happy as a clam. Before I left Harbour Grace, I put that fucking engineering ring in a box in the closet and haven't looked at er since.

"Good for you."

"It all turned out for the better. I landed a job as a counsellor in a group home. I love it. The kids are a challenge but I feel I'm really contributing to the world. To the bigger picture. Doing something useful and meaningful. I'm where I wanna be."

He punched me playfully on the shoulder.

"You always had your act together, Alex. So much more than I did."

He'd always been the popular kid. The one the girls chased. The one the guys wanted on their team for rugby games on the lawn outside residence. The one who'd regaled me with stories of his glory days in high school. I contemplated his sincere brown eyes.

"Arthur James Hopewall, I don't know about that, but I'm glad to hear it's worked out for you. I really am."

He looked at the stove. "Now we gotta bake it for twenty minutes at 375 degrees. Cut the squares while they're still hot."

"But serve cool, right?"

"Right!"

Jackytar

f o r t y
o n e

■

King Christian, the King of Denmark during World War II, insisted the Nazi flag be taken down. He said he'd send a soldier to take it down. The Nazis said they'd shoot him. King Christian said, "No you will not because I will be that soldier."

And they took the flag down.

— Rev. Dr. Brent Hawkes

f o r t y
t w o

∎

Our…creator who art in heaven,
Hallowed be thy name;
Thy kingdom…darn! come;
Thy will be done on earth as it is in heaven.
Give us this day our daily bread;
And forgive us our debts,
As we forgive our debtors.
And lead us not into temptation, but deliver us from evil;
For thine is…dominion,
And the power and the glory,
For ever. Amen.

forty
three

Friday

Telling AJ that I was gay over a plate of date squares and a pot of tea was surreal. After a few blinks and stutters, he seemed to accept it well enough but I wasn't a 100 percent sure if his joviality was a cover. Even so, the experience emboldened me enough to continue asking questions, to keep searching for Maman's cassette and to confront more ghosts from the past.

The day was mauzy, misty and gloomy. Crows squawked on the nearby telephone poles and power lines, but I couldn't see them. They were present but invisible except for their eerie, forlorn noises, their squawks seeming to protest their invisibility.

Then I realized: I knew they were there. They did exist. Even if invisible, their faint yet stubborn sounds proclaimed their presence to those sensitive enough to hear them. I wondered if Dad and Bruce heard them still or had they drifted into an arena of seeing and not seeing, hearing and not hearing, where one's perceptions become blurred and vague?

A dimension of "taken-for-grantedness."

Perhaps my being from Toronto made me see things anew. I showered and shaved and headed downstairs. A familiar smell greeted me.

"G'marnin, b'y. How's it goin?" said Dad, spatula in hand, standing over the stove with his old apron on.

"Excellent. Feeling good this morning," I replied.

"I heard ya up and about and gotcha some breakky."

Dad took a heaping plate of blueberry pancakes out of the oven and placed them on the table.

"You shouldn't have, but thanks. I'm starving. My favourite!"

I put several pancakes on my plate, all made from scratch, buttered them generously and covered the lot with sticky maple syrup.

"Guess my cholesterol level will shoot through the roof, eh?"

"Don't you worry about that. You're young."

He poured himself a bowl of bran flakes with skim milk.

"I don't wanna end up like you. On a diet of oats and cereals and fruits and vegetables. But I will if I keep this up."

He grinned "No worries, as ye says in Toronto. I still likes me salt beef and fish n brews but I made a few changes to pacify Dr. Singh."

We both laughed. Food had always been a central part of our lives in Torbay House. It had always been Dad's main way of showing love; through actions, not words. Jiggs' dinner, fish n brews, figgy duff, fish cakes, homemade chicken soup, and of course, blueberry pancakes for breakfast, fluffy and sweet. All Dad's specialities and Bruce

Jackytar

and I used to love them as much as our houseguests did.

"Dad, can I ask you something about Maman?"

He stopped shovelling the spoonful of bran midway into his gaping mouth and laid it back down in the bowl.

"Well, yis, what's on yer mind?"

I thought about the cryptic, missing tape, *Témoignange*. A witnessing, but of what? What demons from her past had she recorded? Would it uncover the roots of her animosity towards her proper family, or was the missing cassette just another music recording?

"Dad, do you know where Maman kept all her recording tapes?"

He replied without hesitation. "Yup, we got her one a them micro-recorders a couple a years ago for her birthday. She recorded like a banshee after that. Enjoyed it a lot. I believe she keeps —" he paused, "— kept them in her trunk in her room."

"Anywhere else?"

"Probably down at the church. You can check there. Why?"

"I'd like to listen to them. Keepsakes, ya know."

He nodded, but his eyes narrowed. "Alex?"

"Yes, Dad?"

"Be careful what ye wishes for."

"Whattaya mean?"

"Some things is better left alone."

"Like what? Is there something about Maman I should know?"

He looked out to the sea. "Look, I been around a lot longer than youse. I know you and your brudder and Evelyn got more education than I do, but I got experience. I knows the world. The ways t'ings works.

"Yer mudder was a sad case. We done what we could for her. We all did. I couldn't stand the arg'in m'self. Jaysus, I catered to her like a manservant. Handled her wid kid gloves. And she was always cross as a cat. Cept at Christmas. Twas all no good. I mean, perhaps it kept her from killin herself. I dunno. But it almost drove me right off me head m'self."

He'd never spoken so bluntly about her mental illness and the toll it took on him living with her. He stood up, scraped the rest of his cereal into the garbage and started to rinse his dishes.

"Perhaps it all never made no difference. We'll never know now, will we? She had a few good years towards the end. We're all thankful for that. But I knows one thing. Let sleeping dogs lie. She's gone and let her rest in peace."

"I wonder if that's wise? I mean, she asked me to find a cassette in her dying gasp, if you must know. I feel obligated."

He scoffed. "Alex, m'son, she was half out of her mind. Didn't know what she was muttering, if you ask me. Her brain was gone, b'y. Don't pay no heed."

I must have appeared unconvinced, for he sat back down again and said, "Alex, do ya know the story of the Ole Hag of Bond Cove? No? Well, listen ap til I tells ya."

Jackytar

f o r t y
f o u r

■

"The Ole Hag of Bond Cove"

Jessie was ten-year ole when his mudder died. His fadder remarried a widow from in the Cove. She had three children of her own, two b'ys and a girl. They moved into Jessie's house on the outskirts of Bond Cove. Everything was fine for a few months, then the spring came and Jessie's fadder went off to the seal hunt and never returned. The widow complained she couldn't sleep no more.

"The ole hag comes t'visit me," she said.

Now everyone knows what the ole hag is. A witch. She appears as a black poisonous cloud, dressed in shadowy rags. She got a hooknose, beady eyes and warts on her face. When she wakes ya up in the middle of the nigh, yer paralysed. Ya can't move. She sits on your chest and tries to smother ya.

Ya ever have that? No.

Well, the widow was losin her strength. She got so weak she was laid up in bed, but she still couldn't sleep. She called young Jessie into the bedroom.

"I wants ye to do something for me. You'm the eldest."

"Course, Mary. I'll do what I can."

She coughed. "Jessie, everyone knows the ole hag lives deep in the woods beyond Bond Cove, somewhere past the Bog. Ya gotta go. If ya don't, she's gonna snatch me breath tonight, or soon enough! And youse'll all have to go to the orphanage."

If there was one thing the youngsters a Bond Cove feared more than the Ole Hag, twas the orphanage, a bad place in St. John's where other monsters lurked, some more fierce than the old hag.

Twas mid-afternoon when he left. Jessie walked further and further into the woods. Twigs cracked beneath his feet. Rabbits and hares, foxes, blue jays and sparrows watched outta sight. He clutched his little tomahawk tighter in his fist.

He walked and walked. Finally, long after nightfall, he approached the Bog. A steely grey

Jackytar

fog hovered and an owl hooted. He knew he had to go into it and stick to the middle, where everyone knew there was a drang. He crouched down like those shrewd trappers and fur traders that were his people, lookin left and right, cautious of every sound.

At long last, he saw the edge of the Bog. The woods ahead didn't look much more invitin. Most of the trees were crunnicks and covered in maldow. He walked for a few minutes and decided to rest. He awoke to a pain in his chest and opened his eyes.

There she was, the ole hag, the size of a beagle, her clothes black as coal, with beady, black eyes, a face as a pale as clotted cream, a hook nose and a long chin with warts that had hair growing out of em. She cackled and spit, ridin un like a harse. He rose with her into the air until he was level with the tips of the crunnicks.

He could hardly breathe!

He prayed to God above for strength! Then he moved one finger. Then another. Then out of the blue, the ole hag disappeared. He was back on the ground.

He shouted, "Ole hag, I come for yer help. M'stepmudder sent me. Listen ap!"

A wind rustled through the trees. There she was, crouched in a nest of brittle branches.

"What do ya mean?" she screeched. "Me? Help you? Why should I?"

DOUGLAS GOSSE

"Me stepmudder's dyin and she got three youngsters to tend to. She sent me to ask for mercy. I'll do whatever ya wants to save her."

"Mercy, eh? Well, ya got guts, tis sure and certain. Follow me to m'house and we'll see."

The house was perched on giant otters' legs that danced around. Twas made of birch logs wid a roof of mossy sods.

"Come in," she said. "I got three rules. Number one – don't ask too many questions! Number two – do as you're told! And number three – don't poke around! Tomorrow marnin, you'll git yer first task." She pointed to a mound of sawdust in the corner. "Sleep over there."

He slept horrible, wakin up at every creak and groan, for the house wobbled on those giant otters' legs all night. He rose at dawn. The ole hag was nowhere to be seen but she'd left a note on the table next to a bowl of cold porridge:

The stove is cold,
But there's wood to burn,
Lift off the fern,
And remove the mold.

Ya got til night,
Don't dare take flight,
Clave it up into splits,
And you'll be spared m'fits.

Jessie jumped out the door to the ground. Once he'd lifted the ferns away, twas indeed a pile of

Jackytar

wood, much of it mouldy on top. What was underneath was dried out crunnicks. He spent the morning makin splits. By noon, his hands were sore and bleedin. He spelled yaffel after yaffel of staragons into the empty wood box in her porch. This wasn't easy, since the house wouldn't sit still! At dusk, she appeared.

"Hmmph! Ya did it awright," she said. "Now git to bed. Tomorrow marnin, there'll be more to do. Ya got any questions?"

He heeded her warning not to ask too many. "Yup, I got just one...why do ya torment people?"

"I don't torment no one!" she screeched. "They calls me!"

He was surprised by what she'd said but figured twas best to leave well enough alone. He slept better that night, despite the otters' legs on the house dancin around. Once he got up, there was a fire lit in the stove and another note on the table:

I loves me trout,
and sees no more,
Fill up this bucket,
And wash me floor.

There was a line with a hook in an ole wooden bucket. As soon as he wolfed down some porridge, hot now from the fire, he set out. First, he dug into the ground and scooped up a bunch of worms. Then he walked back a ways to the watery section of the Bog, baited the old rusty hook and set out the line. Soon enough, there was a nibble and then another, and another.

He couldn't believe how many trout there were in the Bog!

By early afternoon, the bucket was full to the brim. He ran back to the house in a panic to clean the trout. Then he set about gettin a good blaze goin in the fire wid the splits. He biled some water on the stove. Then he started scrubbin the floor on his hands and knees with his shirt balled up like a rag. Just as he was done, he heard a noise.

"Hmmph, not bad," she said. "Anymore questions?"

"Yis. Why is it they calls for you?"

"They calls for me cause Oi'm the only one they knows will come. Another question?"

He remembered her warning. "No ma'am. Just please leave me stepmudder alone. I clove up your splits. I got the trout. I scrubbed the floor."

She looked around at the shinin floors, the crackling fire in the wood stove and the lovely trout laid out on a dish towel on the counter, ready to fry for her supper.

"Leave now and never tell a soul that ya saw me!"

Jessie didn't have to be told twice. He pulled on his jacket, leavin the rag of his shirt behind in the

Jackytar

bucket and jumped out the door. He walked all night, back through the watery bog, careful to avoid quicksand and puddles that could swallow you forever, through the scary woods, with creatures chirping and ribbeting and howling and hooting. Twigs cracked beneath his feet, makin him peer into the shadows, but not once did he stop. By dawn, he was home. Mary and his stepbrudders and stepsister were happy to see him. He'd been gone for a week, they tole him, much to his amazement, and his stepmudder had slept like a log since he'd left.

The End

"So, what's all that supposed to mean?" I demanded.

Dad leaned back in the rocking chair, smiling enigmatically.

"You think I should go with the flow, eh? Not rock the boat. You think I should let the dead rest. Leave good enough alone. Abandon my search for the cassette. Is that it, Dad?"

He inserted some baccy into his cheek.

"I dunno, b'y," he shrugged. "No comment from the peanut gallery. It's a yarn. Means something different for everyone! You tell me."

forty
five

■

The story lingered in my mind as I showered and got dressed. Should I back off and just let things unfold? Should I ease up or plough forward?

That morning, I helped Evelyn and Bruce rummage though mother's belongings. There was no time to lose. Evelyn had to return to work the next day. There was something odd about rifling through the contents of Maman's dresser and closets. But it had to be done. All the clothes would be given to charity. Maman had some costume jewellery, mostly out-dated and cheap, but there were a few items of modest value she'd received for birthdays, anniversaries and Christmas. Evelyn claimed them.

"You mean she had no will?" I asked Dad that morning.

He fumbled with his teacup. "Naw, no need for that around here. What's mine was hers and hers was mine. Cept for her music room. That was all hers."

Maman had left no will, as was typical among Newfoundlanders of a certain education and generation, but somewhat unusual for someone only in her sixties. But it was in keeping with her sense of *laissez-faire* and therefore not a big surprise.

"So Dad, do you have a will?"

"Nope, never got around to it. Spose I should git one done some day. Not gettin any younger."

"I'll make some phone calls and git you set up with a lawyer," piped up Bruce. "It's important that this git done."

Dad hesitated but then seemed to see the sense of it. "Awright, let me know, m'son. But I don't wanna spend a lotta money."

Trust Newfoundlanders from outport communities to be reluctant to spend money for something their ancestors had never had to do. In the olden days, the era of Poppy Murphy, the youngest son, and his wife if he had one, usually took care of the house and his mother after the father died. Any money, which was very rare, would go to the widow, or be divided up between her and the children if they were grown.

"I'll git ye a fair deal. Don't worry. I knows a few lawyers in St. John's," said Bruce.

"We'll set it all up," added Evelyn.

"Ya haven't got a trunk filled with a few hundred thousand dollars now have ya, Dad?" I said.

It wasn't that unusual to hear of an elderly person dying and relatives discovering such treasure in the bedroom, literally in a mattress or in a trunk. In Bond Cove, such rumours were commonplace. He reddened.

"Naw," was all he could say, confirming my suspicions. I decided to leave well enough alone and to tackle that issue another day. Evelyn and Bruce rinsed out their coffee mugs. They were dressed in smart sports clothing, I noticed.

"You want some breakfast," I asked them. "There's delicious pancakes warming in the oven. Dad made them."

Bruce started to say yes when Evelyn interrupted, "Nope. We're on a diet."

"Oi'm going down to the Government Wharf for a few hours," announced Dad suddenly. "They got a trawler comin in and Oi'm gonna lend a hand to the b'ys."

I was convinced he found it hard to witness Maman's presence being removed from the house and was glad he had an excuse to leave for the morning.

"We better make sure he's set up at the bank, too," said Bruce once he'd left. "I got the feeling he idden."

"Good idea. I bet he has money tucked away somewhere up there. I know he used to have a bank account, though. I saw it years ago when we had guests here. His accounts seemed to be in order for taxes, making cheques and what not. But it wouldn't surprise me if he had thousands just wasting away in a trunk or cubby hole somewhere in the house."

"Let's go do her room, then, alright," said Evelyn, "before he gets back."

We stood in the hallway together outside Maman's music room, as if afraid to enter a tomb. Evelyn dug in her pocket and pulled out the key.

"You have a key?" I said.

"France showed me where it was. No big secret."

We entered. Evelyn peered around, twisting her hands. Bruce looked nervous and out of place in this small room, like an awkward giant in a glass and porcelain shop.

Jackytar

"What do we do with all this?" Evelyn wondered aloud. "Look at all these angels! Pictures, statues, figurines, dolls! What are we gonna do with all that?"

"I dunno," said Bruce as he looked around. "She loved those angels more than she loved us."

I gave him a dirty look, but couldn't really argue with him. Maman's collection of *angelots* had meant the world to her, second only to her pump organ and her music.

Evelyn halted in front of the expensive silver tea service and cleared the tiny cherub dolls I'd left there out of her way. She turned the pot and tray over and studied the engravings, like an antique connoisseur.

"It's so beautiful! Where'd she get this?" she drawled.

"It's been in our family for generations," I said. "Nanny got it from her own grandmother."

The cosy room was crowded with us three big adults standing there. Maman would have been as jittery as a ladybug had she been present. I hadn't been in this room for years and now I seemed to be a regular visitor.

Evelyn gestured at the shelves. "What should we do with the books?"

"That's a tough one," I replied, lifting the garland off a shelf. "Many of these music books are quite expensive and some seem rare."

Evelyn held the ornate little silver milk jug in her hands, as if she'd already claimed it. "Expensive?" she said. "Then what should we do with them?"

"None of us plays the organ, so I think we ought to donate them to someone who can use them," I replied. "Or an organization that will really appreciate them, as Maman did."

"Hmmm. We'll have to sleep on that." She crossed over

DOUGLAS GOSSE

to the end table and bent down to its bottom shelf. "Look, it's France's Bible. How often did she read that? My oh my, you couldn't pry it out of her hands. Alex, we have our own and I know you'd like it. Take it. Right Bruce?"

Bruce nodded. "You're welcome to it. We got a nice one for our wedding. Go on."

I accepted the large Bible and decided to ignore their puzzling, proprietary attitude. On the cover, The Holy Bible was engraved in gold. "I appreciate it. It's a good memento. She used to read this frequently when we were growing up. Wouldn't let anyone else touch it. Thank you. I'll cherish it."

Evelyn beamed magnanimously. Bruce looked so much like a little boy in the room, despite his towering frame. He shook his blonde Anglo-Saxon head. "No problem, brudder."

"And what about the tea service?" said Evelyn nonchalantly, still holding the jug tightly in her fist. "It's old, eh? Out of style. Bruce and I'd take good care of it if nobody else wants it."

"Well, I think we better leave that up to Dad for now. It's been in the family for so long and it's valuable." Crestfallen, she reluctantly put the jug back on the tray. "You have Maman's jewellery, Evelyn, and if there's anything else you'd like to keep just let us know, okay?"

"Sure. No problem. The jewellery's nice." She smiled and I almost believed that she didn't mind. That she hadn't been sarcastic about the jewellery, which contained a few nice pieces including a gold cross and some decent earrings.

Bruce edged toward the trunk and swallowed hard as if summoning the courage to speak. "I think it's a good

Jackytar

idea to donate her music books," he gushed. "But who'd want em?"

I stopped rearranging the garland on the shelf where I had disturbed it. "How about St. Stephen's? I'm going down there later today. I can inquire?"

"Sounds good," said Bruce.

"Sure, whatever," said Evelyn half under her breath, but not before she gave Bruce a dirty look which I caught. She crossed over to the trunk and tried to lift the lid. "Hmmph. I wonder what's in here?"

Bruce got the key out from the hidden ledge under the organ lid.

"Here tis."

Bruce knew where the key to the trunk was kept, too.

forty
six

■

Student variety show and dance. How disheartening. I was trying to round up my class. As I walked away down to the stairs, I heard Julie saying, "That's Mr. Murphy. He's a fruit."

I heard a male say, "He's a faggot." Then, the same male voice called out, "Mr. Murphy! Mr. Murphy! Don't you love me anymore?"

I turned around and saw a strange boy in a baseball cap. The secretary spoke to him, probably because he was loud. I walked toward him and said, "Pardon me?" I was puzzled and alarmed at his boldness and obvious homophobic harassing of a teacher. The small group of boys and girls looked on expectantly. Julie was among them. The boys were from a different school.

The same boy said, "Don't you remember me?"

I asked him who he was.

He said, "Remember me. We talked at Bloor."

"Bloor?"

"Bloor and Yonge. The subway station."

"I don't take the subway, " I said, "Who are you? What's your name?"

He said something like, "David," but I don't know if it was his real name.

I asked him what school he was with and he said something like Birchwood or Beachwood.

I asked him his name again, but it was still slurred.

I said I was going to look for his teacher and he apologized, "I'm sorry," but insincerely.

Julie piped up in his defence, "He's a guest. A friend of mine."

Still trying to round up children from my class, I left them, bewildered and at a loss. I saw the boy in question in the gym again and shortly afterwards he left.

I didn't tell a soul. Who could I tell?

I stayed until after 18h00 and then left, sick to the stomach at yet more mistreatment.

forty
seven

■

After having rifled through Maman's room, we said goodbye to Evelyn. She couldn't get anymore time off for Bereavement Leave. The School Board and the Newfoundland government even attempted to regulate death. She took the bus to St. John's, putting on a tragic face as if she'd been asked to board the boat to hell. The bus stop in St. John's was right next to her door.

I, too, had to return to Toronto Sunday evening. So soon and things were still unresolved. But I had papers to correct in Toronto and lectures to resume. Like Evelyn, I couldn't spend more than these past several days away from my work and obligations. Life went on. Mourning was finite when one had a job, whether psychologically or otherwise ready or not. One thought obsessed me. My visit was drawing to its close and I still hadn't found the missing tape.

After Evelyn's departure, I headed up to my room, the Bible heavy in my hands. I also carried with me some candle holders that had belonged to Maman. I had given two of them to her several years ago for Christmas. They were pewter and gorgeous. The melted wax inside indicated that she had used them regularly and I was glad. The other set was made of fine porcelain and I remembered them from my childhood. Maman had owned them forever and I suspected they had been yet another wedding gift. I made a mental note to ask Dad and Bruce if they minded whether I kept them. After Evelyn and Bruce's bizarre behaviour in the music room, I wanted everything to be out in the open. I laid these treasures on the dresser and sat at the desk, the Bible before me. I hadn't read the Bible in its entirety since I was a teenager. It had been a while since I'd opened one up and read a passage myself, despite my regular church attendance.

It was undeniably a beautiful and expensive volume, King James Version, in black leather and signed at the time of her marriage by her former organ teacher in St. John's. I recognised her name. Maman had spoken of her favourably on numerous occasions. It must have been a gift, a token to celebrate their marriage. In it, Maman had placed several ribbons, bookmarks in fact. I opened to a random section separated by one of the ribbons, to Genesis 25, and started reading the ensuing chapters. The first story I read puzzled me. It was the tale of Rebekah and Issac.

Rebekah gave birth to twins and seemed to have grown depressed. Then Isaac and Rebekah, who were married, pretended to be brother and sister so that men who desired her for her beauty wouldn't kill him to get her. I stood up and laid the Bible on the night table next to my bed. Gulls cawed down by the water, stealing scraps of fish from the waters and I knew the stearins would have flown away to Shepherd's Bluff for the night. I looked out the windows towards the water. Rarely in Toronto could one see such a sight! Toronto had so much smog and the artificial city lights blinded the view of the heavens. But here in Bond Cove thousands of stars, some already extinguished I knew, lit the sparkling ocean.

I thought of Keith and my own obsession with working out. The first few years Keith and I had been together, we went to the gym almost every day together even though we often worked until late in the evening.

"Gotta stay pumped," Keith would joke, half-heartedly, after a twelve-hour day. "Just one more set!"

And I was as bad as him, until he began to party as obsessively as he worked out. Then I had gradually stopped going to the gym, in reaction to the whole cult of body vanity. I read all kinds of literature on the phenomenon and learned a lot. Many women were victims of the cult of beauty but men increasingly, too. And their identity and power was not only constituted by beauty, but embraced in some cases. People knew beauty's pull, its widespread advantage, even if they didn't want to face it for fear of being called vain, superficial, manipulative, or self-absorbed, which they often were. Beauty remained a source of covert and yet overt capital, a segue into positions of privilege, whether in marriages, at the clubs, or firms on Bay Street. Keith and most of his executive friends looked like clones: perfect teeth, tans year round, muscular. You still needed the degrees, the endless hard work and the connections, but beauty increasingly, too. They tended to be tall, these future giants of industry. Some said for every inch over six feet on Bay Street, men

Jackytar

earned an extra twenty grand a year. Indeed, the celebrated conservative store where he and most of his associates shopped for suits catered to tall men. I had gone with him once and at five foot nine, hardly anything fit; they just didn't stock many clothes for the average sized man.

There seemed to be a growing obsession with male beauty, reflecting what Rebekah and Isaac experienced centuries ago. Beauty remained a commodity, something to be fought over and won, yet more than that. Plastic surgery and the less invasive procedures of needles, poisons, acids, and wrinkle fillers were commonplace in Toronto. Few people I knew sported eyeglasses anymore when you could have perfect vision in minutes with laser surgery.

It was no longer enough to earn a six-figure income to ensure a respectable and prestigious place in society. For guys, you also had to look like a winner, and that meant a round butt, a narrow waist, broad shoulders, defined abs, and biceps that could crack hazelnuts. Rates of body disorders among men were soaring, but rather than starving ourselves to death, we strove to be bigger, more muscular, and have less body fat. Like Keith's friend, Carlos, the one that was a cop. Both Bruce and I clearly looked as if we worked out, but he more so than I. I was over that phase and content with two to three workouts a week at the gym, and ski season, to keep me healthy rather than buff. I no longer panicked over a few extra pounds or strove to look like I stepped out of a magazine. I hadn't even missed the gym since my sojourn in Newfoundland.

When I'd spoken to Keith about my theories ages ago, he'd shaken his head, "So what? It doesn't change that I gotta look good to compete! Gotta stay pumped!"

He'd found a new workout partner almost immediately, gone about his workouts as normal and embraced a whole new meaning to partying on the weekend, all weekend. I wondered, not for the first time, if he was also doing steroids, like so many straight and gay men.

I lay down on the double bed and rested my eyes. When I woke up, I was astonished to find that I'd slept for a couple of hours. Dinner was over. I stumbled down to the kitchen and found Bruce sitting there by himself.

"The kitl's biled, if ya wants a cuppa tay?"

"Thanks."

I poured a steaming cup and dug around in the fridge. I took out the plastic container of fish n brews that a sympathetic neighbour had left. I scooped some into a bowl, covered it with plastic wrap and put it in the microwave for a couple of minutes.

"How are you?"

"Awright I spose," he said.

But I had forgotten his reticence. Being around gay men, many of whom were more in tune with their emotions, had made me forget what my brother was like. He'd always seemed troubled by displays of emotions, other than rage or antagonism. As a boy, he was the stoic one, the hockey player. Whereas I'd studied French with a passion, practising with Maman at every opportunity, even going on exchanges to St. Pierre et Miquelon and New Brunswick when I was a teenager, he'd hated our maternal tongue and dropped French after grade nine.

The real boy.

"I miss her, Bruce," I confided. "I wish I had known her better, ya know? The past few years."

Jackytar

"Hmmph," was all he said.

"I was reading her Bible and fell asleep. She had a bunch of red ribbons inserted in certain passages. I read one of them. The story of Isaac and Rebekah. You know it?"

"Yup. That's the one where she married Isaac and then they pretended they was brudder and sister, right?'

I was surprised he remembered, but the religious upbringing we'd had, attending church every Sunday, the Anglican confirmation and the religious symbols in his house, suggested that he might still be a regular church-goer. Evelyn's influence perhaps. Perhaps his own.

"Yeah, then Rebekah gave birth to twins, and seemed to go through postpartum depression. Do you think that's what happened to Maman?"

He stared at his teacup. The silence was uncomfortable.

Death and birth were more closely intertwined than we often thought in society. The one separation popular culture told us to fear the most is the separation of our spirits from our bodies, perhaps because we feared that which separated us from our loved ones. But as Christians, we believed that death reunited us with those who had passed on before us. If that were the case, I prayed Maman had made peace with the family who'd raised her.

"I dunno. How could I? I was just a baby m'self."

I put the bottle of ketchup on the table and dared to share with him some of my thoughts.

"As bizarre as it sounds, I guess that giving birth is a type of entrance into a new world, eh, like death?"

"You have no idea," he muttered.

I took the steaming dish out of the microwave and sat down opposite him. "Whattaya mean?"

His blonde locks glistened even in the dim light from

overhead. How I had envied his golden hair as a child, his blue eyes, his tallness, and his athleticism. He hadn't been a brother, but more of an impossible aspiration. Cane and Abel. I was of average height, stockier, and dark – Jackytar.

"Well, I might as well tell ya. Yer gonna be an uncle one a these days soon."

"What? Congratulations!"

"Hmmph."

"You don't seem too excited about it?"

"Tidden that simple. We can't have youngsters ourselves."

"Okay, I'm confused. You just said I was gonna be an uncle."

He sipped the final drops of tea and set the teacup down with a clang. "We can't have any youngsters. We gotta adopt."

I was floored. "Are you sure? I mean, have you been to doctors?"

"Lard sufferin Jaysus, Alex, we're not stupid! Of course we went to doctors. Fertility specialists. We can't conceive. A genetic problem. She's barren as the surface of the moon. Barren as the Sahara Desert. She had anorexia as a girl and now she can't bear children."

"How do you feel about that, Bruce?"

He leaned back in his chair. "Well, we ain't got much choice now, have we? We decided that we're gonna just adopt, and be parents that way. The whole t'ing's in the works. Won't be but a year or two maybe, tops. We both got good jobs. A secure future. We'll see. Shouldn't take long."

"Congratulations! I mean, I'm sorry that you can't conceive, but adopting a baby is wonderful news! I've thought about trying it myself."

Jackytar

He looked at me with cold eyes and snarled, "You? Yer gonna adopt?"

I was taken aback. I didn't really know if it was a question or a statement.

"Yeah, of course. Plenty of gay couples adopt in Ontario, and some men and women even adopt on their own. I know several. A friend of mine, a chiropractor, just got a little girl. He's so happy. I've been looking into it."

He stood up and violently pushed the chair away. "What's the friggin world coming to? Sick!"

And he left.

Just like that.

The fish n brews cooled on my plate. I emptied it into the garbage bin.

f o r t y
e i g h t

■

Dringgg! I listened to the distant sound of the tide. I was drinking tea at the kitchen table. The wood stove bathed me in a cosy heat. Out there, I knew, was the Atlantic Ocean relentlessly beating upon the landwash.

Déclic!
I recalled driftwood with the profile of a Roman emperor, shaped like a unicorn, a machine gun, and a shark…
I parted the almost transparent sheers.

Dringgg!
I could tell that the sea was there, not only because I heard the crashing waves. No. There were silver glitters from starlight like the shimmering scales of a saltwater salmon.

Dringgg!
I walked into the hallway. Carried the heavy Bible with

me. Next to her room, the old-fashioned black rotary dial telephone vibrated on the little table. The landline had a familiar ring. My cell phone played Mozart and refused to work in Bond Cove despite the phone company's assurance it'd work anywhere in North America.

Newfoundland was like that.

I answered, not expecting a call. Not expecting one from him. Toronto seemed far away.

An alien world that I was removed from now.

He said: Hey, it's me. How you doing?

The flowery cushion shifted beneath me.

I lied: I'm fine. Just fine. You?

Strange.

I looked around.

This used to be my house.

He said: I miss you. I want you to come back home.

I said: Looks like I'll be back this Sunday. Have to tie up loose ends. Sunday night.

I told him about my flight schedule. My stopover in Halifax. Then in Montreal. Words gushed out like a downpour of rain.

I told him about Maman's Bible and the shiny red ribbons.

Leviticus.

Abomination.

Angels.

Deuteronomy.

Sodomite.

As I did so, I traced the engraved letters of the cover with my index finger.

He said: Don't listen to such foolishness. You know

better. Translations of translations of translations.

Weary. I didn't even mention the other passages to him. The other ones that she'd ribboned off.

I didn't even dare speak their name.

He said: Remember the first time we met?

Déclic!

I did. We'd all gathered in the parking lot of the beer store. He'd been so handsome, in his jeans and bulky sweater, so tall. We'd hit it off. Cross-country skiing in unison. Leaving the others to fend for themselves. Even when we'd joined the rest of the group for lunch, we'd only had eyes for each other. The ride back had culminated in a warm hug. The next day, it was raining cats and dogs. Nonetheless, he'd parked near my home and walked in the pouring rain to knock at my door in order to return the thermos I'd left on his backseat.

Flowers couldn't have been more romantic.

I said: I remember.

He said: I cleaned today, too. I know you like it neat. I polished and vacuumed and swept the floors. I'll spruce it up again Sunday before you come so everything's ship shape. I miss you lots.

I wondered about the drugs. Was he still using? Was he still going out? Had he turned over a new leaf?

Some things were best left unspoken until the right time. So I shut up. Too many questions could be dangerous.

I said: I miss you, too, Keith.

He said: I love you, Alex.

Jackytar

f o r t y
n i n e

■

Our creator who art in heaven,
Hallowed be thy name;
Thy dominion...come;
Thy will be done on earth as it is in heaven.
Give us this day our daily bread;
And forgive us our debts,
As we forgive our debtors.
And lead us not into temptation, but deliver us from evil;
For thine is the ki...dominion,
And the power...and the glory,
For ever. Amen.

f i f t y

•

Satur*day*

I slept poorly. At daybreak, wisps of pink, orange and scarlet spread across the harbour to the land and I was overcome with the beauty of it. I made a pot of coffee and spent most of the morning pouring over Maman's Bible, as if by studying it I could categorize and better understand her; however, I found little solace in this scientific method that had served me so well in the past. Perhaps handling the loves and lives of human beings required a more emotional and soulful approach that escaped me for the moment, and I grew increasingly frustrated.

For the umpteenth time, I turned to the family tree where she'd noted the births, marriages and deaths of our Francophone relatives, none of whom I'd ever met. I wondered again why she'd kept us in the dark regarding her side of the family, and I was frightened of the possible answers. The first and last time I'd broached the subject with her, I was about seven years old.

Déclic!

"Maman, who's my other nanny?"

She reacted like a singed cat. "Don't be so foolish. *Tu la connais bien ta grand-mère*, Nanny Murphy! *Franchement!*"

"*Non*, Maman, *Nanny Gabriel, ta* Maman *à toi.*"

"Alexandre Murphy, don't you ever, and I means ever, ask me about her again. Ya ear me! Ever! You ave no Nanny Gabriel. *Juste ta Nanny Murphy.*" She'd risen out of her seat and slapped me across the face. "*C'est tout!*"

She'd looked at my reddening cheek and then at her own guilty hand, that fine white hand with its long tapered fingers, made for playing the organ. She'd turned and looked out the window.

"*Va t'en,*" was all she said.

I fled her room, too shocked to cry.

And here I was almost three decades later holding her family tree, our family tree, in my hands. Bernadette Savidon, my grandmother, married Jules Gabriel and gave birth to four children, three boys, Claude, Jean-Marc and Thomas, and the eldest, France, my mother. She'd also recorded her marriage to Dad and our births. On closer inspection, I noticed something peculiar. She'd taken a pencil and made a neat X over the name of her father, Jules Gabriel, the grandfather I'd never known.

I had more questions than answers. To settle my mind, I decided to take a short walk around the yard. The day was chilly and foggy, but I'd always liked the feel of the minuscule beads of condensation on the exposed skin of my face and hands.

I admired the woodpile. Dad had placed the junks of wood in horizontal stacks alongside the garage and they were as even and straight as could be. The house seemed monolithic beside me, sturdy, and yet macabre thoughts ran through my head, tormenting me. I touched the gummy bark of the snotty var tree Dad refused to cut.

It'll all endure long after Dad, Bruce and I join Maman in heaven, I mused. The secrets of this house would probably remain unknown to whoever occupied it long after we'd gone. Would any of it matter anymore? We were just transitory beings, passing through this life. Maybe we took it all too seriously.

I circled the yard, admiring the tall spruce and birch trees that shrouded the house in privacy. The birdhouse still had guests who were busy squabbling over the birdseed Dad had set out. I spied him heading towards his truck, a rake in his hand.

"Where ya going?" I called.

"Oi'm headin over to the cemetery. Gonna plant some flowers on her grave. Decorate it a bit. Rake the gravel before they brings the tombstone over in the next few days."

"Do you want some help?"

"Naw, I'll tend to it. Bruce is already up there. He went early this marning. You go ahead and do whatever tis you'm doin. Ya only gotta couple a days left anyhow. Enjoy them as best ya can."

"If you insist but let me know later today if I can help with anything else, or just keep you company, okay? I told Evelyn and Bruce I'd go to the church today and clean out Maman's office."

He nodded.

Jackytar

"Dad, by the way, didn't Poppy Gabriel, Maman's father, pass away when she was young."

The words poured out. "Drank isself to death, that man. The hardest kind of an alcoholic. They was better off without the likes a Jules Gabriel. He was known up and down the shore. A proper nuisance that man."

He spat on the ground, narrowly missing his scuffed work boot.

"How old was Maman when he died, then?"

"Jaysus, Alex, that was a lifetime ago. She weren't very ole. That's all I knows. She weren't very ole a'tol."

"I see."

"Why're you askin?"

I told him about the family tree in the Bible. Her father. The mystery of the relatives I'd never known.

"Don't worry about them, Alex," he replied. "Goddamned Jackytars. Not that they're all bad. I've known some fine families, and some fine men, too. Mostly fishermen, lumberjacks and a lot a truckers, too. But her brudders never amounted to much. I mean, I heard one of them got a good job working the highways. He settled down and married and had children. Twas Thomas, I think. Or was it Jean-Marc? Whoever twas, he done awright for isself. I dunno. I think they both did okay, too. Nutten stellar mind you, but they was never in any big trouble.

"That Claude, son of a gun. I knows for a fact he never amounted to much. The lazy lout. Known up and down the West Coast. Just like his fadder. A drinker and a troublemaker. Always gettin in bar fights. In trouble wid the law. Drunk drivin. Public disturbances. One thing after anot'er. Spent some time in Kelligrews at the pen. A proper nuisance!"

He stabbed the prongs of the rake into the ground as if to emphasize his point. This he did subconsciously.

"I used to hear about them from local men that worked up on the West Coast. I'd check up on them from time to time, right, and let your mudder know, although she'd never say much when I gave her news about her brudders. Nor did she dissuade me."

He leaned on the rake handle then and spoke more softly, as if confiding.

"All I knows is this. After our visit up there, France cut off all contact and begged me to do the same. So we did. What else could I a done? I mean, I updated her from time to time when I heard about the b'ys, and when the missus passed on, same t'ing, but nutten more."

He took out a rolled cigarette, lit it with a match and stuck it in the corner of his mouth, all in a practised motion. I thought he had quit smoking, although I knew he still chewed tobacco, but I said nothing. Maybe the stress of the past weeks had gotten to him.

"Listen, m'son, I'll tell ye once more. Yer mudder wasn't right in the head half the time and the other half she was crazy. Alex, yer m'son and a grown man, so do as ya likes. But I'll give ya one word of advice, okay? Let sleeping dogs lie. Sometimes the past is better buried in the past, s'all."

Déclic!

"Dad, one more thing."

"What's that, m'son?"

"Why'd ya get yourself mixed up with some crazy 'Goddamned Jackytar' anyway?"

Jackytar

With that he turned his back, took a puff of the cigarette and then flicked it on the ground. He flung the rake in the back of the truck and took off not even bothering to look back. I was left standing there in the trail of the truck's exhaust. A trawler was heading in and a crowd had gathered on the Government Wharf.

Maybe Maman's secrets were best buried with her in the cemetery?

But I had to find out for myself.

fifty
o n e

■

I gratefully inhaled the saltwater air. Everything seemed
grey, the walls, the wharves, the sky, the cars in the parking
lot, and the pathway.

Le soir, tous les chats sont gris!

I slipped further away from the commotion inside,
leaving AJ and the girls behind me. I neared a marble
fountain out back in the middle of a discreet garden. My
shoes crushed frozen grass underneath, but I was drawn to
the eerie beauty of the statue spouting water from an urn
held in well-shaped hands, the hands of a poet, a pianist, or
a painter. Water cascaded from the urn into a basin of
half-rotted twigs, dead bugs and bits of earth. Touch. I
tentatively traced the firm jaw line of the statue, over
patrician nose, bee stung lips, Adam's apple.

Fearfully, I peeked around. I was alone. Trembling
fingers feathered protuberant pectorals, hard nipples, down
to washboard abdominal muscles, over gentle love handles.
Entranced, I stepped to the left, and allowed my hand to
graze wonderfully rounded buttocks. A flutter in my groin.

"I wish you were alive," I whispered, wanting to kiss that statue on his frozen lips, not daring to. If someone saw me.

Sitting on the marble bench in front of the marble god, cold permeated my butt and thighs. I hugged myself, placing my hands in the warmth of my armpits. I chanted a private prayer I'd only said before in the privacy of my bedroom.

A cracking branch interrupted my erotic reverie. I feigned nonchalance. It was the handsome barman, emerging from a path in the brush. He had been giving me the eye all evening. Nervously, I returned his smile.

"Well, Hercules, we meet again," he said.

"Hey, how ya doin?"

"Oh, I was talking to the statue!"

I smiled. He sat next to me and draped an arm over the backrest. "I had to get some fresh air. The smoke and noise were gettin to me. Name's Jamie."

I shook his hand. It was warm and soft and yet firm. "Alex."

"So you go to university?" he asked, leaning closer.

"Yeah, first year. French."

"Cool! I'm doing a Master's in biology but I work part-time in clubs to pay the bills."

"I waiter sometimes."

"Cool." He looked at me attentively all this time, making me feel fuzzy, hyper and ill at ease. "So, ya gotta girlfriend?"

"Not really." I thought of the trio inside and tried some light banter. "Haven't met the right one. I guess."

"Alex, you're really good-looking. I mean it. I'm impressed."

"Thanks." I traced a circle in the wet gravel with the toe of my shoe. I wanted to tell him how gorgeous he was, but the words stuck in my mouth.

"Ah, these university parties are such a bore. Same ole, same ole. But it pays the bills. And sometimes I get to meet someone really cute. Like you, Alex."

I laughed but even to my ears it sounded self-conscious and awkward.

"Not much of a talker though, are ya?"

"I dunno what to say. That's all," I stammered.

"Look, I gotta go. Missin out on all the tips. How about I give you my phone number? We could go for coffee sometime."

"Sure! That'd be cool."

He scribbled on a scrap of paper from his wallet and handed it to me. His touch lingered for a few seconds until I pulled my scalded hand away. He grinned. My heart thumped as loud as the music inside long after his silhouette had faded from sight.

I returned to AJ and the girls and confided in no one. I never called.

Jackytar

fifty
two

■

I left a message for Rev. Byrne to call me back. When the phone rang at noon, I was surprised and pleased to hear AJ's voice.

"Hey, how are you doing, buddy? How's the family?" he said.

"Oh, Evelyn returned to St. John's yesterday so Torbay House is stiller than ever. I gotta leave this Sunday myself. Dad and Bruce are off working in the cemetery, fixing up Maman's grave. So I guess we're doing tolerably well. Life goes on. Bit by bit, we're getting everything straightened away."

"Did she have much stuff to go through?"

"Not really. She was pretty frugal in her spending. We got her clothes ready for the Salvation Army to pick up. Mostly she had music books, but some are vintage. Quite rare and expensive. We agreed to donate them to St. Stephen's. I hope they can get another organist or pianist. I'm just waiting to hear back from Rev. Byrne.

I want to clear out Maman's office at the church so Dad doesn't have to bother. He's a bit crooked with me today."

"Why's that?"

"Oh, he made this stupid, insensitive remark about Jackytars and I asked him if he had felt the same way about Maman."

Silence for several seconds. "Why'd you do that?"

"Well, I was reading Maman's Bible. She had all kinds of passages marked. Strange stuff from the Old and New Testaments about marriages and deceit," I said vaguely. "It got me thinking about Poppy Murphy and his exploits."

"Yup, he was a Irish rover, that one."

"I guess I reacted without thinking, given the circumstances, but it was just too much."

"That happens, Alex. Don't beat yerself over the head with it. From what I remember you sayin, your grandfadder was pretty racist, wasn't he?"

"Yes, he was, but Dad's a good guy."

"Well, he's a grown man. He can handle it. A lot of that was a sign of the times. We know better today, right?"

"Right. There's no question."

"So can I help clean out her office? I'm free by late afternoon and all day tomorrow."

"Certainly, I'd appreciate that. We can catch up some more. And more hands make for lighter work."

"Alex, it was nice catching up with you. Reminiscing. And the date squares were excellent." He paused. "Just like old times."

"Likewise AJ and I'm glad I told you about Keith, too. It's important for friends to be open with each other."

"I agree, Alex. No sweat." His voice turned sentimental.

Jackytar

"I'm honoured you trust me. Like I trust you. There's something I've been meanin to tell ya, too."

"Oh yeah? Well, shoot. No time like the present."

His voice rose. "Nope. I want to keep that for a one on one. Don't fret. It's not bad."

"Okay, I guess I'll have to wait and see." He had always been so intense when we were students. Nothing appeared to have changed in that respect. "So what are you doing today?"

"I'm at the home. Just finished a counselling session with a young fella who had some trouble in the past. Trouble that still haunts him."

"Oh yeah?"

"Yup. Christ, Alex, some of these kids have no kinda family life. This kid's father left when he was a toddler. His mother's on welfare. Alcoholic. She was known up and down the shore! Had a string of boyfriends. The last one used to abuse him, the court says. He claims they both did. They ran a porno site on the Internet. You might not know it, but as many women as men are involved in that. He ran away. On the streets of St. John's. Doing drugs and drinkin. In with the wrong crowd. Same ole story."

"It happens a lot, eh? There's thousands of street kids in Toronto. Lots are gay and lesbian. Kicked out by their families. Forced into prostitution to survive. It kills me to walk by them on the street."

"Yeah, if only we'd invest half as much money in school and child care as we do in sports or beer or cigarettes or cable television, or politician's salaries and perks!" AJ said.

"You know, the most opulent buildings in Toronto are the corporations and the tallest of those are the banks,"

DOUGLAS GOSSE

I said. "Marble floors. Extravagant materials and furniture while many downtown schools are destitute. Lots of poor kids don't have enough books in their classes or even good lunches. And many downtown children are ethnic minorities and lots are refugees. The independent schools do, though, where the rich send their kids for $15,000 to $30,000 per year. In many of those schools, every kid has a laptop. Can you believe that? Private tennis courts, running tracks, swimming pools, and baseball and football fields are common. Some of the elite schools even have horse stables. Week long ski trips and school trips to Europe, South America and the Caribbean happen every year. And they often cap class size at fifteen or twenty, but classes tend to be smaller than that. All children should have equal access. It's disgusting!"

"Well, it's been years since this kid lived with his abusive mother and her boyfriend, and now she wants to rekindle the relationship. She only got a suspended sentence, ya see. The court didn't believe she abused her son. She testified against her boyfriend in return for leniency. Crazy! The poor kid can't handle it. All the ups and downs. The roller coaster ride. He was cryin in my arms. Beggin me not to make him go through all that again."

"What are the child's right, eh?"

"Exactly, what are the child's rights? And the system treats him as a juvenile delinquent. He acts the way he's been taught. No more, no less. If he were a girl, we might a been able to git him into a nice foster home. But nobody wants a troubled thirteen year old b'y."

"That's a tough one, AJ. I'm sorry to hear that he's going through so much. Your job must be really tough on you. How do you cope?"

Jackytar

Silence.

"Well…it is a tough job, but I know I'm makin a difference in the lives of these youngsters. That motivates me. I go to every conference and seminar I can. There's lots of alarming studies and trends. 'Family violence' has become synonymous with 'violence towards women and children!' There's hardly any specialized clinical training programs to treat male victims anywhere. And of the almost 4,000 children in custody today in Canada, most are male. It's friggin frustrating, but I do what I can."

"Why are there so few programs for them?"

"Part of the problem is that many boys and men are ashamed to admit they've been abused. Doubled with that, they may be disbelieved if they do summon the courage to tell someone. And if the problem isn't known, we can't create programs. Then there's little money for the programs that already exist and more and more cutbacks. So some fear gettin an even smaller piece of the pie if we also focussed on males, see?"

"Oh what a tangled web we weave," I said. "I'm glad to see you've got so much passion and conviction."

"Well, life's short. Someone once told me that."

I pictured his earnest eyes.

"Now I've pontificated enough," he said. "Are we on for cleaning out her office, then? You'll call me?"

I rose from the telephone desk. My knee creaked. I looked at the time on the grandfather clock.

"For sure. I'll call and leave a message as soon as I hear back from Rev. Byrne. Shouldn't be long."

"Great! I look forward to it. And then we'll talk some more."

"You'll tell me your… 'secret'?"

"You bet!"

Not for the first time since I'd arrived in Bond Cove, I wondered about AJ. Was he interested in having more than a friendship with me? When we were both students, I had wanted nothing more. Now I wasn't so sure.

Just as I was getting ready to have lunch, Bruce appeared in the hallway.

"Can we talk?" he said.

Jackytar

fifty
three

∎

"What do you want?" I said, perhaps a trifle coldly.

My brother's face was half shadowed in the dim light cast by the chandelier. According to Dad, Maman had insisted on low lights once we no longer took guests. She claimed it soothed her and that the blaring lights were too much for her eyes. Bruce looked upset. With his Anglo-Saxon stoicism, I had learnt to interpret minute twitches of the lip or facial muscles, a slight downcasting of the eyes, as opposed to a forthright sneer or frown. His body dared betray few emotions, even in times of duress.

"Let's go into the kitchen and have a mug up," he said, leading the way.

"Where's Dad?"

"Still at the cemetery. He'll be down soon enough. Alex, I wants to talk to ya about what I said, ya know, about you adopting."

I reached into the cupboard for salted crackers as he plugged in the kettle.

"Okay, sure, we can talk about that. So what's the problem?"

I took some cheddar cheese out of the fridge and laid it on a plate with the crackers. Next to the butter. Real butter.

"Well, I should apologise, first of all, for what I said." He swallowed. "I was a real jerk."

"Well, brother, as if it wasn't hard enough to be gay in this world, to have my own brother tell me I wasn't fit to adopt was a slap in the face I didn't need."

"Hey, I'm trying to bury the hatchet, okay? Gimme a break."

I shrugged off his apology.

"I didn't think you could be so petty. You know, Bruce, I've worked with kids for years. I'd make a great father. It shouldn't matter that I'm gay. And it shouldn't matter to you, my own brother. Christ, I'm sorry Evelyn and you can't conceive, but I was congratulating you for crying out loud."

"I know what I said was wrong. I was blowin off steam. Listen, can I tell ya something?"

I nodded.

"I hates to admit it but Oi'm a bit jealous, I guess."

"What? Jealous of me?" My eyes must have bulged. "That's a new one. Whattaya mean?"

"You livin up there on the Mainland. All the freedom."

I stared at him in wonder. "If I remember correctly, when you worked in Alberta, you couldn't wait to come back home?"

"I was only nineteen. Workin in construction. A shit job. Decent wages but shit hours and the boss always breathin down m'neck. All I did was work, work, work! I'd

Jackytar

have a buddy or two for a few weeks, a month maybe, and then he'd git fed up and move on! There was no union or nutten like that. We was treated like friggin slaves."

The kettle started whistling. He poured our tea. We both added milk and sugar.

Still stung from his homophobia, I felt like shouting, "And does not a fag drink tea?" "Hmmm. The best tea around," I said instead, lapsing into big brother mode and regaining my composure. "Always tastes better in Newfoundland. And when someone else prepares it." He stirred his cup for too long. That always annoyed me. "Now tell me more. I'm listening. I didn't realize it'd been so tough."

"Ya didn't ask."

"Well, I was in university," I countered. When he'd returned to Bond Cove, he'd flashed his money around like a log baron, boozing and staying out all night, ridiculously dressed up in a Western cowboy hat and boots. Good God! Maman and Dad had been at their wit's end. "Bruce, I had no time for much anything. I was working part-time as a waiter and studying my ass off at university in St. John's."

"Hmmpf!"

There it was again, that nasal, explosive Newfoundland sound of disdain, contempt and frustration.

"What does that mean?"

"You're always talkin about your rights. About not havin the right to do this and that. Jaysus, I wish I could do what you does."

"Huh? You gotta be you kidding!? I can't even walk down the street with Keith without fear of being gay bashed. Or by myself for that matter. Even in Bond Cove." He flinched at the mention of my partner's name. "Yeah,

Keith, my partner of eight years. We've been together longer than you and Evelyn, but were we ever invited here? No. Did you ever make a move to include us in family holidays? No."

He sipped some tea and apparently scalded his mouth.

"Fuck," he said quietly. Like Dad, he poured the hot tea into his saucer in order to cool it. "Listen, brudder, I don't recall you ever mentioning wantin to come down to the Rock. You hardly ever called or emailed. Seems to me twas you cut us off."

The coolness in his voice caught me off guard. He seemed to have thought about this more than I would have given him credit for. I wondered if there was any truth in what he was saying. Had I indeed cut us off from the family? Could I have visited with Keith? Would they have welcomed us?

"You're always going off to some foreign country, Alex. If I remembers correctly, in the past few years, let me see," he counted on his fingers, "Australia, Taiwan, New Orleans, New York…London? Did I miss anywhere?"

"Yes, you did. I also presented at conferences in Chicago, Washington, Los Angeles, Halifax, France, Germany, and lots more. All work-related. If you had gone to school, you might have been able to travel a bit more, too."

He leaned back in his chair and sipped tea again. "I swear, Alex, sometimes you're as deaf as a haddock! Ya can't see the caplin for the shore! You saw the way they drove me. You saw the way I was pushed. I was supposed to go to the national leagues. Be a Canadian hockey star. That was supposed to be my life, right? You don't understand the pressure I was under."

Jackytar

The rite of hockey practises and games night after night, and even at the crack of dawn, from October to May in particular, that was his life and Dad's, too. The weekend games. Dad chauffeuring him all over the island. The championships on the Mainland. Dad's pride. Maman's meek enthusiasm and congratulations when she heard he'd scored or assisted, the most she ever gave anyone.

I spoke slowly, measuring my words. "I thought you realized that was just a pipe dream?"

I detected bitterness and disappointment in his blue eyes. He smoothed a stray lock of blonde hair back from his forehead. He hadn't hit the hair gel yet today for the first time, perhaps because Evelyn was gone

"Nope, not until it was too late. That's all they lived for, Fadder and Poppy Murphy especially. The teachers. Everyone in Bond Cove. I had the weight a their expectations on m'shoulders. I spent my teenage years being the hero, the hot shit in high school, until I came to the conclusion that I wasn't good nuff. After years of everyone tellin me I was. Dangling that carrot before my nose. Twas silly! Hardly anyone is. I mean, I could've continued wid the minor leagues in St. John's and I did for a while, but I'd never be drafted."

He slurped the cooled tea from the saucer into his mouth. I thought of my own experiences in high school. Immersing myself in my studies. Escaping to St. Pierre and Miquelon as an exchange student for several months in a French Lycée. Always trying to fit in. All the parties and classes and events that were geared towards straight couples, as if gays didn't even exist. It was hard for me to feel compassion for him.

"On the other hand, you spent yer time studying.

Workin to git away from here." He wiped his mouth. "Now who's better off, eh?"

"Bruce, I'm sorry. It hasn't been a bed of roses for me either, ya know. I don't earn much money. Your house is far nicer and I'm sure you have more savings. Keith earns the money in our relationship and what's his is his."

"Money isn't everything," he said.

"True."

"Yeah, well, when you're told that you're the next best thing since sliced bread and then you realizes it's all bullshit, well…yer world starts to fall apart, see?"

I didn't want him to get away with his prejudices so easily.

"Bruce, it's still no excuse for disrespecting me for wanting to adopt a child," I said. "It hasn't been easy for you, but try being gay. You can't even walk down the road without fear of getting beaten up. You can't work without fear of someone treating you like shit. You're laughed at and excluded in a million little ways day in and day out. Sometimes it's more subtle, but it's there. I'm always on guard."

He took a bite of a cracker with cheese and spoke with his mouth full. After all these years, he still did that.

"Try havin little or no education and tryin to land a job. Or land a girl, even worse."

"You did alright, no? You've done fine with your construction work. Your carpentry. Better than me."

"Yeah, ya might say that. Oi'm a decent carpenter and the construction work keeps me goin. But my back is startin to bot'er me something awful. I'll survive for a few more years I spose, until it gives out. Then I dunno what I'll do."

Jackytar

Unemployment and worker's compensation, I imagined, but kept quiet.

"And Evelyn?" I inquired.

"I hopes ya never has to go through what I goes through," he said. "She thinks Oi'm beneath her. A caveman. Stupid and ignorant. Neanderthal she calls me."

"So why'd ya her marry, then?"

He sucked up the remainder of the tea and looked beyond me, out the window. He sought answers, or perhaps solace, in the Atlantic Ocean, too, I saw. He rose and rinsed out his cup.

"It wasn't always like that! When we first met, I was still playin hockey in St. John's. I knowed her brudder. I'd stopped drinking and finished trade school. I had a good job. He introduced us. I was the captain of the team. Rakin in the cash. I bought that house ya saw for almost nothing. For a pittance. Fixed her up real nice.

"Things was goin good the first few months. I thought I'd found the girl a m'dreams. We got engaged. I bought her this big diamond ring. When I asked her to marry me, I was surprised when she said yes." He took another cracker with cheese. "Then after the wedding, things turned sour. Fast. She says it's because we can't have a baby. I told her I didn't care about that. We'd adopt. Besides, she started actin different right after the wedding before we even knowed about that.

"The house was fixed up exactly the way she wanted it and then I had a patch where I couldn't work. I injured the disks in me lower back and was laid off for a full month." He beat his fist on the table. "Jaysus, I wonder why I ever did it? Why'd I git caught up in that mess? It was like she hated me. She used to complain about earning all the money. I was getting unemployment insurance, but that wasn't enough to please her. She was worried about what her friends would think and her family. She never said I was lazy but that's what she thought. She treated me like I was a bit a dirt from between the devil's gnarled hooves!

"She'd come home and I could barely move the first while, laid out on the broad of m'back. I'd hear her clankin the dishes around downstairs, stompin around. Then she'd come to the bottom of the stairs and call out to me to come and git m'supper. I'd somehow manage to stumble down the stairs and we'd eat at the kitchen table. You could cut the tension wid a knife and then we'd start arg'in. Day after day. Nothing I did, sir, was good enough for her. She was crooked all the while she cleaned the house or did any of the chores I normally did like taking out the garbage, shovelling the driveway and clearing away the dishes. I went back to work after about three weeks even though m'back wasn't healed. Just to shut er up. I couldn't stand it no longer. And m'back's never been quite right since, but she don't give a fuck as long as the cheques keeps rollin in."

"And now you might adopt?"

"Alex, she drives me off me friggin head! I'm like a proper angishore! She says she'd like to give up teachin full-time and raise a baby. Maybe work half-time or be a substitute teacher. I knows she'll have me out working fourteen hours or more every day a the week if she can, to keep the clothes, the *saalonnn* appointments, the house!"

He looked grim.

"She earns a good salary, top of the scale as a teacher, but I do earn more. But by God, I slaves for it. Sometimes I feels like a bloody workharse, I do. One day, I'll drop

Jackytar

down and I won't git up no mar. Then maybe I'll have a bit a peace. Oh, and she wanted Mudder's gold locket before we planted er in the ground! She would a yanked it right off er neck if I hadn't a stopped er! Didn't know that now did ya?"

"Bruce, this is so surreal." I wanted to hear Evelyn's side of the story. I'd witnessed her admonishing him like a child, chiding him, but I'd thought he deserved it. He could be self-centred and selfish, or so I'd thought. A doubt nagged at my mind nonetheless. "You didn't actually give it to her, did you?"

"No way! Hmmpf!" That sound again. "Ya should've seen her a couple a nights ago. We had a wicked argument the night before she left. Mom's tea service, ya know, the silver one in her music room? Evelyn said she should git it because she's a woman and no one else would value it. I tried to tell her that it belonged to Dad now but she wouldn't take no for an answer. She told me I'd better hit him up for it before I came home.

"Then she wanted me to drive her to St. John's in the car. She wouldn't drive herself. She got a license same as me. Said I should be a gentleman. Jaysus, Alex, I drives all the time and whose the gentleman for me? I gotta do it all by m'self. No one's ever gonna chauffeur me around, unless I ends up in a wheelchair, which is entirely possible.

"So she packed up her gear. Throwing her stuff around. Rippin mad about takin the bus even though it delivers her practically right to our door and she could a taken the car. All crooked as ole hell about the tay service.

"She says, 'Watch him. He'll take the tea service back to Toronto.'

"I says, 'Evelyn, don't worry about it. Mudder's not

even cold in the grave. I got work to finish here wid the grave and such.'

"She finally quieted down when I told her I wanted to keep an eye on ya to be sure ya didn't cart the works off to Toronto wid ya. That seemed to pacify her."

The thought of pillaging Maman's meagre belongings was laughable. Could Evelyn really be so cunning and paranoid? I kept my mouth shut. I'd never heard such a long speech from him in my entire life and I wasn't about to put the damper on it.

"I told her there might be a bit of money from Maman's death if she'd pipe down and let me stay til Monday. I told her we'd let ya take care a the music books to git on yer good side. That took some convincing. She had it in her mind to cart em all off to St. John's and sell em in a used bookstore. That old one down on Duckworth Street. Ya knows the one? I had to convince her to let you donate em to St. Stephen's in Mudder's memory. That they was more trouble than they was worth and we might wing the tay service yet."

He stood up and peered out the window. The black crows squawked on the telephone pole. Waiting, waiting, watching, never leaving. A vigil none too silent.

He sighed. "I misses the days when I was doin up m'house, workin farty or so hours a week at m'job, workin evenings and weekends on renovations. But I was happy enough. No one to bother me. He-yeah. Playin recreational hockey. Just for fun. For m'own pleasure. Hangin out wid the b'ys. They was a good gang. Not a bad apple amongst em. Evelyn seemed happy, too. We had good times. Now m'back is too sore to even skate. I works around the clock. M'backs gettin worse and worse. I wears

Jackytar

a brace at night. And Evelyn's like a drill sergeant. She don't love me no more. Only what I brings to her financially and workin around the house."

"I'm sorry, Bruce."

"So how can we go ahead and adopt a child? She says it'll make us stronger. I dunno what to do anymore. Leavin her is frightening. She already swore she'd take me to the cleaners and git the house. I loves that house, Alex. I can't start over. Too late for that now. I haven't got the health or the strength."

He shook his head dejectedly.

I patted him on the shoulder and muttered, "Bruce, it'll all work out, b'y."

Comparisons with Keith flashed through my mind. Keith earned far more than me, but although it was his condo, purchased with his down payment, we both paid half of all expenses. But his crazy behaviours, his induction into the cult of body vanity, drug ridden nightlife and glitz reminded me of Evelyn.

Greed.

Appearances.

Capital gain.

"Bruce, have you tried talking with Evelyn. Really talking?"

He loomed over me like a Nordic giant, his lip quivering.

"Sure ya can't win, b'y. Ya can't! Ya knows what some women tends to be like. They brings up stuff from two year ago. Four year ago. Stuff I can't even remember sayin or doin. Evelyn can talk circles around me. That's all she and her friends spends their time doin. Talkin for hours on the phone. Yakkin in the kitchen or in the livin room. Drinkin coffee and talkin. Shopping and talking. They looks at me like Oi'm a big loser. They used to like me. She got em turned. A caveman. She calls me that, ya know? Maybe she thought she could turn a sow's ear into a silk purse when she married me, I dunno.

"Tis a dog's life, Alex. A dog's life. Oi'm trapped like a lobster in his shell. Dropped into a pot of bilin water. Unable to git out." He looked me straight in the eyes again. "Alex, b'y, Oi'm not really homophobic. I knows you'd make a fine fadder. Better than me, probably. You got the education. You're a sensitive guy. Ya got a good heart."

Déclic!

He craved my support.

One question burned in my mind. The words flooded out as if one long string of syllables. "Bruceattheendofyourlife, whattayathinkyou'lllookback-onasimportant?"

He understood.

"Not this, Alex. Not this."

He looked out over the Atlantic Ocean in resignation, perhaps? Suddenly, he shook his curly mane of blonde hair, as if trying to clear his head and surprised me by saying, "Alex, you knows French…what was that expression Mudder always used to say all the time? *On responde oez imbeciles —?*"

I was astonished that he remembered any French, let alone that expression. He hated it with a passion in school, dropped it after grade nine and steadfastly refused to speak it with Maman. "*On répond aux imbéciles par le silence?*"

"Yeah, that's it, brudder. Sometimes silence is the only thing a fella from around the bay got left."

Jackytar

fifty
four

■

Our creator who art in heaven...
Hallowed be thy name...
Thy...dominion...come;
Thy will be done on earth as it is in heaven.
Give us this day our daily bread;
And forgive us our debts,
As we forgive our debtors,
And lead us not into temptation...but deliver us from evil;
For...thine is...dominion,
And the power and the glory,
For ever. Amen.

fifty five

■

Sunday

I got up early. Checked the answering machine in the hall-way. Still no response. Ate breakfast. Fried eggs. Toast from homemade bread. Hort jam, the blueberries harvested from Bond Cove's very own marshes, heaped on. A special treat. Gulped strong coffee. Not tea. Did the dishes by hand. Swept the floor. Went to Maman's room. Started to open the door, then stopped. Turned away. Climbed the stairs. Looked at the beautifully bound Bible. Lay on the bed. Opened a passage separated by a red ribbon. Read and reread, riveted. Genesis 4:26; 5:3-8. My brown forehead wrinkled in consternation. Then Genesis 19:4-11. I opened yet another section. Genesis 20:12. Frowned. Minutes flew by, turned into an hour, two.

I rang up the minister.

"This is Rev. Heather Byrne. I'm not available at the moment. Please leave your name, number and a short message, and I'll get back to you as soon as I can. Beeeep."

I stuttered. "Hh…hello, Rev. Byrne? This is Alex Murphy. I called you a couple of times since the funeral. I have to return to Toronto this evening, so I really need to get into mm…Maman, I mean Mom's office today, okay? I also need to talk to you about something important. I can't talk over the phone…something's worrying me. That I don't understand. Concerning Mom. Perhaps you can help me? Could ya please…call me bb…back, as soon as possible? Thank you."

I opened the Holy Bible and read again. The ribbons were so stiff and untarnished, but the sections had been studied many times. Studied by her. Exodus 6:20; Numbers 26:59; Leviticus 18:9-22; 20:13-19.

My feelings hard to ascertain.

Shock. Puzzlement. Revulsion. Confusion?

Ancient voices. Voices of old. Romans 1:26-27, I Corinthians 6:9 and I Timothy 1:10, Deuteronomy 23:17-18. Voices that did nothing to quell my sorrow and consternation. Voices that troubled and disturbed.

I laid the Holy Bible on my stomach, which now ached. I twisted my head to the right and then to the left, and heard the muscles scratching. I stared at the upside down golden letters scrolled on the cover until I got a headache. Closed my eyes. Exhausted. Started to nod off. Tossed and turned. Dreams troubled me. I looked around the room and out the window.

Opening my eyes did me no better.

Like this I remained.

f i f t y
s i x

■

I wanna be with you

I wanna *feel* the sunlight warm your shoulders
Like I did once before
the memory remains potent
magical
and feverish

I wanna *taste*
the sweetness of your breath
as you hungrily devour my kisses
wonder in your eyes before
during
and after

I wanna *hold* you close
your supple body melting into mine
as I lick the salt from your nape
(even if it tickles you)
and awaken next to you in the morning

I wanna lay my head on your chest
listening to the crescendo of your heartbeat
keeping time
a lazy soul lullaby

> I wanna be with you when
> rain pelts the earth
> sun dries the rain
> and tears course down your cheeks
> so I can wipe them
> *with my fingertips*

I wanna *sense* you in all that I'm worth
Be there for you
stimulate you
As you do me

> I wanna anticipate your thoughts
> collect your wisdom
> caress your ego
> uncover your mysteries
> and softly (like a butterfly)
> brush my lips against yours
> *delicious*
> gently travelling down
> further and further
> past all resistance

> *I wanna be with you*
> I want you

DOUGLAS GOSSE

fifty
seven

∎

I snapped the Bible shut and headed downstairs. I looked anxiously at the grandfather clock. She hadn't called yet. Time was drawing near. Tonight. Leave this behind. My childhood. Maman's life. The mysteries of Bond Cove. The pain and suffering. The familiarity of home. Close the book on all this, this paradox that was my life no more and yet still enslaved me…I stood transfixed, staring at the locked door of her music room. Minutes went by. A lifetime.

Déclic!

And I made a decision. To leave the house.

I walked down Murphy's Hill to St. Stephen's Church. Crows stared. Watching me. Tearing apart my movements. I stumbled down the paved driveway with the shrub guardians. Waded through the fog. Last night it had rained. Small puddles of water where the pavement was sunken. Foggy as smoke in a Labrador tilt. Fog encasing the House. Fog barring the Atlantic Ocean from view. But I could sense the salt water. Smell the fresh, briny kelp and the pungent odour of gutted fish that the westerlies carried over the land and up Murphy's Hill to Torbay House.

Familiar smells!

Down the hill. Past the colourful saltbox houses. Past the modern bungalows that younger folk had copied from suburban developments. Those who hadn't permanently fled to St. John's or the Mainland. Incongruous in this setting.

Like me.

Ernie Lundrigan passed me on the street.

"Howzit goin, b'y?" the old man asked, winking and making a clicking sound in his cheek, as Newfoundlanders do.

The old man wore standard issue for his generation: blue coveralls, a khaki jacket lined with orange material and a navy tam like my father's. A rolled cigarette dangled from the corner of his mouth. He was carrying an ole paint splattered bucket, work gloves and a knife. On his way to the Government Wharf no doubt. A whistle. Trawler coming in. He'll be gutting fish soon with the other men for the rest of the day. Good way to earn a few dollars, what with Christmas coming up.

"Fine," I responded softly, then looking ahead, carried on at an even quicker pace.

The steeple peeked through the fog. Sundry feelings and then memories.

Déclic!

Choir practise as a boy and the shrill sopranos of the older ladies. Shyness as I had to go in front of the altar at the Christmas concert, holding up a large picture of the donkey that carried Mary to the manger, and sing. I'd searched for my parents' faces in our pew and seen how anxious they looked.

Would I mess up?

St. Stephen's glowed eerily in the mist. The doors formed an arc. I took the knocker in my hand, a thick steel ring, but stopped mid-air before actually rapping at the door. I tried the door and it opened soundlessly.

"The hinges are well oiled, that's for sure," I said aloud. "Now let's see what's up in here."

I walked into the narthex, my footsteps echoing, and stood at the threshold of the sanctuary.

Déclic!

The awful, boring sermons of my youth. If I started getting agitated, they'd give me a peppermint knob and reprimand me quietly. I might be sent to my room later.

Dad always prepared roast beef, chicken, or Jiggs' dinner for Sunday dinner after church. Lovely food that would have tasted great if it hadn't gone down in lumps. Maman was often brittle, ready to snap. She'd scurry off to her music room to play the organ or listen to Wagner's *Valkürie* for the thousandth time.

Father'd take off outdoors to socialize with his buddies down at the Government Wharf or in some fisherman's store. They'd work on an engine, or mend a criss-cross fence. Bruce and I would squabble over the dishes, but usually I washed and he dried. Then Sunday afternoon would be free to do whatever I pleased. My tension would dissolve. Except when she blasted that cursed Wagner opera again and I'd hear it through the walls. I used to wonder why she listened to that dark opera so much.

Jackytar

Now I knew.

I had to face it.

While Bruce scurried off to play street hockey with his friends, I'd read my treasured books. My portals into fantasy, adventure, power, possibilities, and life outside. Beyond Bond Cove lurked a large world, ready to be discovered, with endless possibilities!

Sometimes, I'd timidly knock on her door. She was always mildly surprised when she opened the door and saw me there, as if it took her a moment to recognize her own son, her own flesh and blood.

"*Entre, mon p'tit,*" she'd say, after a pause. "*Sois prudent avec mes angelots*! Mind m'little angels!"

We'd speak our language together. Our private tongue. She'd show me some of her new music books, containing masterpieces by Duruflé. Widor. Vierne. I'd be careful not to disturb any of the pictures, figurines, or dolls, her *angelots* as she called them.

She preferred French organ music to English.

"*C'est ben plus beau. Ben plus beau la musique française,*" she'd explain, talking slowly and firmly, as if it were not open to debate. And with her, it wasn't. It was the way things were.

She'd tell me how she longed to play them on the pipe organ at St. Stephen's, the beautiful organ by the Frères Casavant de Québec. Her beloved pump organ in Torbay House wasn't sophisticated enough to be able to play much of the complicated music she loved. That required several keyboards, not just one, but Aunt Flo was a witch who wouldn't let her practise enough. She cherished the books anyway, humming and trailing her long, elegant fingers over the scores while listening to recordings. Sometimes she became so engrossed, she'd forget I was there.

Then she'd look at me and say, "*T'es encore là, toi*?!"

Whether it was a statement or a question, I never knew.

I knew she'd fret and be displeased until she was allowed to practise them here at St. Stephen's. At that very organ in front of me.

The bench empty.

"Can I help ya, sir?" said a woman, startling me. She was carrying a bucket and cleaning supplies, evidently on her way home. She wore a long coat and a homemade knitted cap hugged her skull. She crept forward and touched my hand with familiarity.

"I knows you. I knows you, don't I?" She looked me over from head to toe with rheumy green eyes but there was nothing insolent in the action. "You'm Alex Murphy, Julian and France's boy."

"Nice to see you, too, Mrs. Barrett. It's been a long time."

"Well, you'm hardly a boy now, is ya? All grown up. A man."

"I hope you didn't mind me coming on in?"

"What odds about that! Tis good to see ya again. Years. It's been years. Ever since you was in high school, I spose." A look of regret crossed her face. "Oi'm so sorry about your poor ole mother, m'ducky. She was a good woman. A real treasure to the church. I meant to talk to ya at the wake but there was so many people about."

"No problem, Mrs. Barrett. I understand. And how are you doin yourself?"

Jackytar

"Right as rain. Harold passed away four year ago. So I'm on me own, but keepin busy as a nailer! Keeps me goin. I still works here at the church, see. Cleans the church for Rev. Byrne."

"I'm sorry. Were you on your way out then?"

"Yis. Just finishin up for the day. Gotta git home and see to the cats. Left em alone all day. Ginger don't like that much. The other one, Snowball, he don't care. Anything I can help ya wid fore I leaves?"

"Yes. I need to get the things from Mom's office. Clear it out a bit. I'd come back later but I'm leaving tonight."

"No problem, m'ducky." She pointed. "Rev. Byrne's down there now anyways. In the vestry. She'll lend ya a hand. Take care now, m'love."

She squeezed my arm and walked past me, this woman whom I hadn't seen in twenty years, who touched me and talked to me with such kindness, like I was family. I walked down the aisle, perhaps the only church procession I'd ever know, other than a funeral. Red carpet and the sweet smell of dust, old people, faded flowers, and burnt incense. Fragments of Christmas Eve as a boy.

Déclic!

The adults loomed above me like giants. The pews were full. The scent of ladies' perfumes and men's aftershave lotions. A good smell. A clean and happy smell.

Excitement because Santa's coming tonight!

I remembered walking up the aisle to our spot near the front, holding hands with Maman. Only the minister's family and the Pierces were seated closer to the altar than we were.

"Closer to Gawd!" Poppy Murphy used to joke.

Dad looking handsome and somewhat uncomfortable in his grey suit and red tie, his hair glowing like the halo of an angel from a biblical storybook at the Bond Cove Medical Clinic. They always dressed us alike; two brothers, one blonde, one brunette, wearing argyle sweaters, buttoned up shirts and grey pants. People smiled as we walked down the aisle. Maman smiled back, timidly holding my hand.

My cheeks burned. She held my hand tightly in her own. We made our way to the pew like royalty. She was wearing a fur coat and pearls that showed off her dark hair and olive complexion…

I looked down at our pew, empty now, and the stillness of the church engulfed me.

Déclic!

I vividly recalled the fleeting pain across Maman's pretty face when Aunt Flo started playing during services, fumbling over some of the notes that she could play effortlessly. I felt her pain then. I relived it now. A stabbing in my gut. I'd never stopped feeling it really. The pain of this Jackytar mother. Just like I carried the pain of my father. And the pain of the million insults, jabs, punches, and kicks that were etched into my soul. I hadn't forgotten all the pain, even though I pantomimed through the daily routines, the performances and the charades of being male: a man, a teacher, a son, a brother, and a lover!

I still carried it with me.

I might not speak its name all the time, but it was there, whether the world acknowledged it or not…

Jackytar

Déclic!

Maman's hands and feet discreetly play a phantom organ. When the singing begins she stands and we sing joyfully. She nudges Bruce to join in. But he doesn't like singing. Dad's baritone is smooth and sure. Maman and Dad look at each other. Dad reaches out his hand. She briefly caresses it, before pulling it away, a rare sweet gesture –

I touched my silent cell phone, carried in the small pocket of my jacket out of sheer habit. Keith. Some deal with the pain in different ways. A light from the geometric windowpanes flickered across my eyes, causing me to blink. I reached the vestry and heard movement inside. I knocked without holding back and announced myself.

"Rev. Byrne, it's me. *Alexandre Murphy!*"

For some reason, I said my name with French pronunciation.

Silence.

"Rev. Byrne, I know you're in there!"

Rev. Byrne opened the door. Her face as round as the bung of a cask. She forced herself to smile. Stuttered when she spoke.

"Alex, I meant to…to call you. Pleas…please come on in."

There'd been too much silence in my life.

In hers.

Time to break the silences!

DOUGLAS GOSSE

f i f t y
e i g h t

■

The vestry had changed little over the years. The walls were still painted a nondescript taupe. Hymn books and Bibles covered the table at the rear, but there were some new additions. A digital clock on the wall. A large Monet print of a picnic. A throw rug underneath in navy blue with red polka dots. Choir gowns still hung from wire hangers on a rolling garment rack of gleaming aluminium. And then there was the far right hand corner. I knew it was Maman's niche right away, for it carried the same stamp as her sanctuary at home. An oval picture of a blonde cherub hung on the wall at eye level if you were seated at her desk. I recognized the wooden desk immediately, for it was the desk of all my teachers during thirteen years of schooling in Bond Cove Public School. They had always seemed to me symbols of the power of knowledge and education, these solid desks behind which teachers graded and planned. Being called up to the desk sent the heart skipping. Maman's desk was scuffed but polished, likely salvaged from the old school before a new regional one had been built a few years back. The argument was that by having bigger schools which served several small communities instead of just one, the Avalon Peninsula could provide superior facilities and resources to students. Above Maman's desk and the oval cherub picture, someone on the vestry committee, perhaps my father, had installed wooden shelves. These were lined with more of Maman's music books, compact discs, her *angelots* and, I could see, another rectangular black leather cassette case, a twin of the one at home.

"I tried to contact you."

She looked grim and guilty, her brown eyes shifty. "Yup, I know. Please have a seat, Alex."

She shuffled over to Maman's desk and indicated the chair. Although the desk was ancient, the chair was a modern swivel model with a supportive back. I put my backpack on the floor alongside the desk and sat down. She lowered herself into the ordinary wooden armchair next to the desk. When she looked at me directly, the butterflies doubled in my stomach. "Alex, I'm very sorry about your mother."

"I know."

"And we need to talk." Her voice sounded more confident, as if she had resigned herself to our conversation and was even relieved.

"I know." Pause. "Rev. Byrne, we'd like to donate Maman's music books to St. Stephen's.

"Please call me Heather. I'm not one for titles."

"Some are quite rare," I continued enthusiastically. "A variety of well-known organ composers. Verne. Widor. Duruflé…if you want them?"

Avoidance. As usual, I was pre-empting a difficult conversation with niceties.

"Thank you but that's not really why you're here now, is it?"

The question was rhetorical. I bent down and opened my backpack. I pulled out the beautiful Bible with it's golden lettering and expensive leather cover, the gift she'd received on her marriage from her organ teacher in St. John's, over thirty-five years ago. Heather nodded ever so slightly as I laid it on the table.

"How about we tackle the easy parts first?" she said, laughing. Laughter is so hard to define and doesn't always indicate mirth. This laughter could best be described as kind resolve. "I figured that would come up," she said, indicating the Bible with a flutter of her hand. "Had everything all marked out, then, did she? I'm not surprised."

I stared above her head at the music books, recognising names. Bach, of course, and her favourite Canadian composers, Healy Willan, whose English Romanticism she listened to fanatically, and the strange harmonies of Gerald Bales and Barrie Cabena, whom she admired for their imagination and innovation even if she closely guarded her own.

"She was obsessed with homosexuality," I stated, cutting to the chase. "She read these passages over and over again. I can't imagine how many times. Thousands? I can't understand what made her so obsessed. There's other passages, of course, but let's start with those." I choked. "She rrib...ribboned them off, these biblical scriptures about homosexuality and she poured over them for years, maybe daily. I don't get it. Why was she so tortured about it? About me?"

Jackytar

Rev. Byrne shifted in her chair. The rolls of fat jiggled and cascaded down her belly onto massive thighs. "I know. I know it's hard for you to understand. I know it's a shock, even, and I'm truly sorry."

"Can you help explain?" I asked, the desperation in my voice alarming to my own ears. The stoic male façade was crumbling. Fear gnawed at my guts.

Rev. Byrne's breathing seemed laboured, no doubt due to her size, but I suspected there was more to it than that. She, too, was fearful, unsure of how to proceed.

"I can try, and —"

I cut her off, "And there's a tape miss…"

She raised her finger to her mouth to silence me. "I know. I know all about it. Patience."

Rather than reaching for the cassette case on the shelf above our heads, she tottered over to a locked filing cabinet. She took a key from the chain around her neck and opened it, speaking softly.

"I had wanted to keep it hidden. But I see now that wasn't my place. I was wrong. Initially I suggested she make it as a sort of therapy. She was too uncomfortable to talk about it with Dr. Singh, or in great detail with me, so I suggested she write her story down or record it." She retrieved an envelope from inside, returned to her seat and tore it open with a sigh. "She chose to record it, of course, being a musician. She never intended for anyone else to find it. Especially not Julian or Bruce."

"She asked me to find it when she was on her death bed," I said.

"I gathered as much. She used to call you *le professeur*. She was proud of your accomplishments in education. Especially that you taught French."

"I don't know if she ever told me that."

"Well, she often said it to me. She always kept me up-to-date after you'd call. Said you had ambition. She was glad you were making a life for yourself on the Mainland. That you were better off. And one day about a year ago she told me she'd made the cassette and hidden it away in her trunk.

"When she became sick, I couldn't get the cassette out of my mind. France shut herself up in Torbay House and wouldn't return phone calls or receive visitors. So the day we brought her into St. John's for good, I dug around for it in her music room. I was afraid someone else might stumble upon it. But it wasn't there! I thought I'd have a heart attack. I'm not cut out for being a spy. Then I found it here in her desk. Thank God." She reached her hand into the envelope and put it on the desk, between us. "Here. You deserve to know. To hear her side. You're her son."

I stared at the small tape – *France Gabriel, Témoignage*. I reached for it. She stopped me.

"No. You have it now and you can listen to it shortly, but let's begin with the scriptures on homosexuality. I think that's best before you listen to the tape. Okay?"

I suspected she had rehearsed this in her mind many times. I could scarcely believe the tape was there before me. My quest was almost over. I'd fulfill Maman's dying wish. My shoulders began to relax for the first time in over a week.

"Fair enough," I agreed. "It'll be heard, her story, whatever the content and consequences. So what can you tell me about all this?" I indicated Maman's Bible. "She must have thought I was a sinner. Damned to hell, I guess, eh? And I suspect she blamed herself. And all the other references to, you know –"

Jackytar

She raised her hand to silence me. "One thing at a time, okay?"

I sputtered but obeyed, having decided to put myself in her hands.

"Alex, I'd like to say upfront that this is one of the hardest situations I've ever confronted. Now that being said, I want ya to know that I apologise for putting it off. Yup, I'm truly sorry for that. I was wrong. A coward I guess, as much as I don't like to admit it. What we say here tonight will leave both you and me changed human beings forever. And we both have to be okay with that. This isn't an easy conversation for either of us, but I want you to know that I'm here now, to listen, to dialogue and to support you, okay?"

"Heather, I'm grateful. These past few days have been…troubling. I'd really like to get some answers."

"Alex, I don't know if I have any answers but I can provide some perspective. Is that awright?"

"Sure," I said.

"Okay, so let's start with the word 'homosexuality.' It didn't even exist until about 1869. Did you know that?"

"I did. My pastor, Rev. Dr. Brent Hawkes is a social activist. He married the gay and lesbians couples. It was in the news? I was there that day, expecting a bomb to go off at any second or a shot to be fired, and look where we are now." She looked at me with interest, cocking her head slightly to one side. "The word 'homosexual' was coined before heterosexual, I believe. Then the medical, legal, educational, and," I smiled at her, "religious institutions got a hold of it. A new identity was created based on sexual orientation. Homosexuality became treated as a disease until the medical establishment decided it wasn't any longer. Or at least enough of them to have it changed. That sound pretty accurate?"

"Sure is. There were all sorts of treatments for homosexuality. But they just don't work," she said. "Being gay has become more accepted, more acknowledged. Except among the religious wrong, the fundamentalists, including the Roman Catholic Church, the church your mother grew up in and never really left."

"I think you're right," I said. "I think she carried the infamous Catholic guilt with her day in and day out."

"He-yeah. Oh I know she did! We talked about that more than once. Her guilt was deep. As deep as her shame and suffering. We're moving forward but we have a long ways to go regarding sexuality in this society. Many clergy don't understand the genealogy of 'homosexuality' in the Bible, or sexuality and gender in general, and that's what I'd like to discuss with you now as a segue into your mother's situation."

I nodded.

"The biblical languages, Hebrew and Greek, had no words for heterosexual or homosexual, so it's deceptive when homosexual is translated from a biblical text. It's wrong to proclaim a biblical view on 'homosexuality' since the term didn't even exist until the late-nineteenth century. And while there were what might be called same-sex or homosexual behaviours back then, referring to them as such is really wrong without understanding the society of the day.

"Alex, as far as we know, Jesus never said a thing about homosexuality; however, he did speak on God's unconditional love. The Bible is more about love and acceptance than pointing out people for blame, hatred,

Jackytar

or sin. Now France has sectioned off certain scriptures here, huh?"

She retrieved her glasses from a pocket in her sweater, took them out of their flowery padded case and perched them on the edge of her nose. I began to see why a recluse such as Maman might have opened up with encouragement from Heather. She opened the Bible.

"He-yeah. Deuteronomy 23:17-18 is really about temple prostitution, not homosexuality or sodomy. Genesis 19:4-11? Let's see. This one is very interesting. The men in Sodom may have intended sexual abuse of the angels but it's unclear. Besides has anyone ever looked at an example of heterosexual rape as the basis for saying all heterosexuals are evil? It just doesn't make sense. And I've never heard anyone preach a sermon on Lot offering his virgin daughters to the mob as a sin. Tisk. Tisk."

"Those are good points," I said. "But what about Leviticus? Everyone always quotes Leviticus. Especially the fundamentalists."

"Ah, yes, my favourite," she joked, turning to Leviticus 18:22; 20:13-14. "These verses really disturb me. He-yeah. It says here that children who misbehave should be brought to a field and stoned! But the reference to men lying with men as with women relates to patriarchy, you see? Women were property back then, not seen as human beings, like in Canada and Britain not so long ago, where-as men were believed to be made in the image of God. We merely came from a man's rib if you refer to Genesis and take it completely literally! So you see, a man lying with another man would 'reduce' him to female status, in that sort of misogynist view." She peered at me over the top of her glasses and raised her eyebrows.

DOUGLAS GOSSE

"Misogyny and homophobia are closely linked then," I said. "Both are fear and hatred of the feminine, whatever that is." I hunched my shoulders. "But what about Romans?"

She ran her finger thoughtfully over the passage. "He-yeah. Romans 1:26-27. The only passage which seems to address homosexual behaviour among women and men. You need to look at the whole chapter though. Paul is talking about idolatry. People who put other things before their devotion to God. You see, the homosexuality he uses as an example is idolatrous, something that the fertility cult worshippers practised. You can't generalize that to other homosexual activity that isn't part of ancient fertility cult worship."

I was pleased at her sharing views on the Bible in such a scholarly way. I had a burning question. "Heather, did you ever discuss these passages with Maman?"

She closed the Bible and sat back in her chair. "Yes, indeed I did. We had long discussions more than once, but it was taking time." I waited expectantly. "Alex, your mother had other demons persecuting her. Ones that drove her to close her mind. To think that she was being…punished for something she had no control over." She paused. "You see, Alex, I have personal interests in this. I'm also gay."

This came as no surprise to me. My gaydar had gone off the moment I'd met her.

"Heather, it can't be easy for you. In your position?"

She squirmed in her seat, her face a puzzle of conflicting emotions.

"Alex, it's been real rough being pastor here at times. Especially first off." She laughed self-consciously. "I wasn't

Jackytar

always this huge. The bigger I got, the less they asked me about why I wasn't dating. Until they stopped asking altogether. And there aren't many lesbian bars or clubs here, so I tend to eat. A lot."

I thought of Keith and his constant dieting, health shakes and compulsive workouts. And then the music and the drugs. The sex.

All to escape.

To cope.

To numb.

An illusion. A trap.

"It's a funny thing. The fatter I became, the more invisible I was. Maybe that's not the right word, but they stopped pestering me about 'the nice young man from New Harbour' and 'the young widower in Heart's Desire who lost his wife to cancer.' You know how annoying that can be? They finally left me alone. I suppose they thought that no man would ever want a fat woman and they were probably right."

"Heather, I can't imagine how it must be for you in Bond Cove. I tried it and I had to leave. Couldn't hack it anymore."

"Real rough at times. But there are advantages, too. He-yeah. I spent a few years in Toronto, you know."

"Really?"

"I did my divinity degree there and got ordained. Then I felt an urge to return home. A call to the sea, you might say. I hated the subway. I can't say I appreciated the skyscrapers. Or the smog. Or the onus on material possessions so many seemed to have. And I love the salty fresh air in Bond Cove. The yarns the old timers tell me. The fresh bread they send over to the rectory. I love serving their spiritual needs as best I can. And you know, there's a lot fewer baptisms than funerals. I guess I feel a sense of guardianship. And of belonging, too. So maybe one day I can come out to my congregation. But not yet.

"But I want you to know one thing." She hammered her fist on the desk. "Picking and choosing scripture to negate human rights is not my style whether it's to support the oppression of women, to endorse slavery, or to prop up homophobia! The Bible is about love and acceptance, not intolerance, ignorance and bigotry. I know I'm not the best example of what I preach, but I also believe that everyone's circumstances are different."

"I know," I said. "I've had a similar dilemma as a teacher. There's no pat answer."

"Alex, on the bright side, your mother came out of her shell and really contributed to the community. For that we should be grateful. I meant every word I said in her eulogy."

"I only wish I'd been able to share more of the joy with her. But they did a good job keeping me at arms length. And I thank you for helping her…" I searched for the correct word, "rebirth. It was really something to hear, but…what about the other passages…the ones we haven't discussed?"

My words came out slowly and evenly but began to deteriorate as my dread grew. I took the Bible in my hands and opened to the other sections she had ribboned. "Isaac and Rebekah, who pretended to be brother and sister, right? Why did she care about those stories?" I flipped to Genesis 4:26; 5:3-8. I almost knew the passages off by heart, having poured over them so often in the past

Jackytar

couple of days. "And Seth, who must have married his sister, or perhaps a niece? It makes no sense to me!"

From a distance, I heard my voice rise like a stearin high above, then sharply descend.

I turned to Genesis 20:12.

"Look! Abraham married his half-sister Sarah. They had the same father! And God apparently let them. Here," I pointed out Exodus 6:20, Leviticus 20:19 and then Numbers 26:59, "the parents of Moses, Aaron and Miriam were nephew and aunt!" I was practically ranting then but couldn't stop. "It says such unions were later banned by the Law in Leviticus 18:9–14 and 20:17,19! What happened? What does it all mean? Why did she read these horrible stories over and over again, until the pages are worn like the taps of a beggar's shoes?"

Heather's face glowed with sweat, betraying her stress. But her voice when she spoke rang clear as a bell. "Alex, what you have to do next is hard but I want you to listen to her tape and try to remain calm." She laid her hand on my shoulder. "Alex, you must."

Her soothing voice jarred me out of my mounting hysteria. She withdrew her hand, took off her glasses and placed them in a case before putting them back in her pocket. "It's about a half hour long. I'll be waiting just outside. You can come get me at any time, okay? I don't know any other way to do this, Alex. Just know that she was suffering. You've already read the passages, Alex," she gently patted my hand, "so you know already, don't you?"

I glanced at Maman's beloved music books and nodded in stunned silence. Heather's eyes were brimming with tears. Finally, I spoke.

"Yes, I know. I think I've always known."

I took Maman's tape player out of my backpack, and in the heat of the moment, decided not to use the headphones. Heather left, closing the wooden door gently behind her.

Time to clue this up once and for all.

Maman's familiar voice filled the silence.

I braced myself.

And listened.

Jackytar

fifty
nine

■

Dad was taking the rake out of his truck when I returned to Torbay House with a box of Maman's possessions. He watched me climb up Murphy's Hill.

"I spose yer goin soon, eh?"

"Yup. In another couple of hours. Got a late flight."

"I'll drive ya in."

"I'd appreciate it."

"Are ya awright? Ya looks a bit pale," he said.

"I'm a bit tired, but I'm fine. I just got Maman's stuff from the church. Just a few things."

"Oh, yeah?"

"Yup. Some toiletries. A scarf and gloves. A few pictures and knickknacks."

He took out a picture and held it in his hands.

"My, that was last Christmas. Just one year ago. Hard to believe."

"Here today. Gone tomorrow."

"Alex, what ya asked me about yer mudder wasn't true," he said suddenly.

"No?"

He leaned on the side of the truck and looked out at the Atlantic Ocean, seeing what I saw. Dories tied to small wharves. Gulls circling around Government Wharf. A few men working in their yards. Clothes hung up to dry in the brisk autumn wind. A scattered car driving around.

"Alex, I'll never forget the first time I saw France play. She'd kept it quiet. Secretive. This talent a hers. This day, oh, I spose we had been datin for a month or more. She said she had somethin to show me.

"She was actin all timid and nervous. But I couldn't drag it outta her what it twas. She insisted we go fer a walk. That she'd show me. She took me down to the church. Twas like a cathedral. Oak pews. Gigantic chandeliers. The argan pipes hidden behind grates. Built in 1930 by the Casavant brothers in Quebec. She told me there was over two thousand pipes. The keyboards even had proper names. There was stained glass windows of Jesus and different biblical scenes!

"I can't describe it all to ya, b'y. Can't do it justice. T'all felt different with her music swirlin about me for the first time in m'life. Her playin was special. Physical and spiritual. Hands goin. Her feet doin a jig on those pedals. Her brown eyes blazin. She was mine and I was hers. From that moment on."

He gestured in the direction of her music room. At the *oeil de bœuf* window she must have gazed out from often.

"Love isn't rational, ya know. Nope. Not rational a'tol. We t'inks with our brain, but we loves with our heart."

Jackytar

s i x t y

■

"A Mariner's Poem"
(so you may always remember)

When first we met, a friend I sought,
And didn't expect the love you brought,
And tho' the winds assail our ship's mast,
We know we can survive the blast.

In the present we do dwell,
Around the chimes of the evening bell,
Whilst soon the anchor must be cast,
We know our love is meant to last.

And on we float and wait and love,
We might yet find our destined cove.

For love such as ours is meant to be,
We'll take the test and ride the sea.

sixty
one

∎

Time to stop living in the past!

– Alexandre Murphy

s i x t y
t w o

∎

I study Bond Cove from my vantage point on the peak
of the hill. The poplar and fir trees flourish around
St. Stephan's Anglican Cemetery. In the distance, gulls,
seemingly as small as nippers, only grey-white, batter the
water by the Government Wharf and fight for fish guts.
Their squawks carry far. The colourful saltbox houses
seem quaint. I face the granite monument erected for my
grandfather, Skipper Murph. I used to read books here in
the summertime. It is a tall, solid Celtic cross with a bronze
plaque. Skipper Murph had insisted on a quizzical epitaph:

> As I am now, so must you be:
> Therefore prepare to follow me,
> As you are now so once was I
> Therefore, prepare yourself to die.

I reach into my jean pocket, extract two shiny coppers and

throw them on the grave. They bounce and settle.

I then turn towards Maman's adjacent grave and kneel. A laurel wreath bears the inscription, "To my beloved wife, France Murphy."

"He didn't know," I say aloud, "or did he?"

I breathe the fresh, salty air deep into my lungs. Then I place my backpack on the ground beside her tombstone. It's blank and won't bear her name yet for several days.

I take her Bible out and lay it on the cold grass. Next, I pull out an old spade wrapped in a cloth from my backpack. I cut out a sod in the space between their graves, about one foot square and delicately place it aside. Then I dig. When the hole is deep enough, I lay her Bible in there. I use my hands to fill it up with earth. Next, I smooth over the ground and carefully replace the sod, fiddling with the sides, so it will look untouched.

"*J'espère que tu as de la paix maintenant, maman. Je te pardonne. Que tu me pardonne aussi.*"

I wipe my hands and walk away. I close the metal cemetery gate behind me and refuse to look back.

Jackytar

sixty three

■

Post*lude*

There's one more thing to do. Shepherd's Bluff. I walk alone. Past the saltbox houses. Past the landwash. Ole Man Howell is mending a fence in the north corner of his yard. He must be ninety if he's a day. He waves. I walk along Brigg's Road. Idly kick at a rock on the dirt road. It's Sunday, so the dories are anchored to individual wharves dotting the harbour. I squat down at the edge of the cliff and climb down the mossy drang. Seagulls fly overhead and I'm mindful not to step in bird shit. Rocks and pebbles roll to the bottom in my passage. But I'm surefooted. I've climbed down here more times than I can count.

At the bottom, I halt, startled.

Someone is seated on My Rock, arms resting outstretched, facing the Atlantic Ocean!

"Good afternoon, Alexandre," he says. He rises and walks towards me.

"AJ, what are you doing here?"

"I knew you'd come. I had to see you. You didn't call me back. We were gonna go to the church together."

I reclaim My Rock. "Well, I couldn't call. I couldn't get to the church until the last minute." AJ sits alongside me on a boulder. We're both quiet for a time. "I'm leaving in a few hours."

"I don't want you to go," he murmurs, arms folded across his chest. It's freezing down here with the north winds rolling in off the glacial Atlantic waters.

"Pardon?"

"I don't want you to go. I love you."

I stare at him and then at the ocean. "I see."

Waves assault the rim between the water and the shore, lapping at the red rocks, incessant erosion over thousands of years, for thousands more to come. I wonder when they came here, how did the ones like me cope? And the ones who had lived here for eons before they came?

"Say something."

"I don't know what to say."

"I know you love me, too."

I look at his silky hair, the trembling mouth, his intelligent, caring eyes. How I used to long to share my feelings with him when we were in university, so young and full of hope and promise. I was miserable when we were apart. I used to pray to God for a way to keep us together forever.

"I'm sorry, but I can't."

"What do you mean? We can make a life together. Move to St. John's. Start over together. Far away." He takes my hand. I let him.

"Far as ever a puffin flew, eh?" I mumble.

Jackytar

"Pardon?"

"AJ, I have a partner. His name is Keith."

He doesn't skip a beat. "Are you guys married?"

"Nope, we're not."

"Well, are you happy?"

I withdraw my hand. "I'm committed to him."

"Then what odds! Git on with it! Put him behind ya! You don't love him anymore, right? Come with me. I always wanted to be with you. Secretly. But I was afraid. It took me time to find out who I am. What I want. What I need. And that's you, Alex Murphy. You're what I want and need. Please."

I think of Heather Byrne. Mrs. Kyle.

"You can't be gay here, AJ. They won't let you. Unless you hide. Unless you're silent. And even then, you betray yourself unless you're married with children, a wife and a picket fence. I can't go through that. I lived that when I was teaching in town. No more."

He looks hurt and protests. "But times are changing. It's not like it used to be. We could live in St. John's! We could be happy there. I know we can work it out."

"I've lived there already, AJ. I know what it's like. I was a teacher, remember, and now I'm in teacher education, okay? They get at you in subtle ways. It won't work out. Unfair student evaluations. You don't get tenure. You have to work twice as hard as anyone else to prove yourself. You can't network with your gay and lesbian colleagues because they're closeted and afraid and many of the feminists distrust you because you're a man. It's like that in Toronto, too, but at least there I have more freedom than in town. More anonymity, too. I can even talk about homophobia in my courses sometimes, as long as I tie it in with race and gender. It's a better life. As long as I keep my feet firmly planted on the ground."

I throw the empty husk of a sea urchin into the sea. They cover the flat rocks here.

"Tons of Newfoundlanders like us move to Toronto and go crazy, AJ. Can't cope. Some miss home. Some become promiscuous after so long in hiding. And you know what that can lead to. Lower self-esteem. Disease. Death. Some drink too much. Drugs. The whole party circuit lifestyle. It can end badly. I've seen it. But it's still worse here on the Rock. At least in Toronto I've got a chance. I want to live. And I want as good a life as I can get in this world. I'm trying. Giving it all I got. I plan on making it. Day by day."

"Some do manage in town," he protests. "Lots even!"

"I can't."

AJ rises and throws a rock into the harbour, skimming it several times. He turns and faces me again. "I refuse to believe we can't make it together, Alex."

He bends and we kiss. How I used to dream of such an embrace with him. It's a kiss that romantic movies would envy. I feel his love. Fireworks. A million stars burst. We separate.

"I have a question for ya," I say.

He looks optimistic, his familiar, cocky smile returning. "Sure, anything."

"Are you out to your parents? At work?"

His smile turns to a frown. "Nope. I'm not and I can't be. I take care of them. They're getting older. Christ, Alex, you should understand. I work with troubled youth. I could lose my job. All it takes is for someone to call me a fag. To lie and say I touched him and I'm out the door!

Jackytar

I couldn't handle it. And my parents are traditional. You know them."

"You've answered your question then, and I do understand. But I can't live like that. Sorry."

sixty
four

■

My ears are plugged and I'm chewing gum to alleviate the
pressure. I look back over what I've written the past week.
I'm astounded by the gamut of emotions I've run and the
secrets I've uncovered. The tape was her dream catcher. It
helped her filter out bad memories, bad dreams, purge
them from her tormented soul.

Tragic.

Maman had given birth when she was a teenager.
The town mayor, the husband of her organ teacher,
had fathered this child. They'd left it out on the porch
overnight to die. In the cold.

That tiny infant she'd never held.

Tragic.

Estranged from her family and town, this sixteen-year
old pariah. She fled to St. John's to start a new life. And
try she did. Unexpected love. Marriage to a good man.
A gentle soul. A hard worker with a tender heart. A perfect
match, she'd thought. And the two baby boys she'd given

birth to and cherished. One as dark as herself. One as blonde and rosy as her husband.

She had loved them both equally.

Then the drive to see her family on the Péninsule de Port-au-Port.

L'incertitude.

The extending of an olive branch. Hope and anticipation. An opening to reconciliation. To another new beginning. Then the horror of her mother's admission regarding her paternity. Disbelief. Shame. Powerlessness. Retreat into herself. For there was nowhere else for her to go. Nothing she could do, or say, to fix it. And her atonement. What she thought was religious penance. Punishment by staying with Dad, living with him in Bond Cove for years and years. Separate bedrooms. No more love and sharing.

Or did they?

And was that what had frightened her the most?

I'd never know.

The people around me look like regular people. Heading off on vacations and to the Mainland for work, to resume their lives, like me. I sing the paradoxically cheery lyrics in my head:

Tall are the tales of Newfoundlanders on the sea,
And Skipper Murph's were the tallest you ever did see.
He sailed upon the Bona Vister,
A better cap't did never exist, sir!
Ahoy, ahoy, de diddle di deh

I don't know if it was all true or not. Perhaps Maman suffered from delusions. Perhaps her own mother had lied to her. Perhaps *grandmère* had also been mentally ill.

DOUGLAS GOSSE

Parfois la réalité dépasse la fiction.

Fiction and reality mingle, overlap and form obstinate beliefs in some when what really matters are the lessons we learn and the questions, not the certainty or the blame.

At least she had her music, both before her meeting with Rev. Byrne and after. All her tapes were dream catchers really. Her music had worked magic in tandem with her *Témoignage* in her final years, liberating her soul, setting her freer than she had been for a long, long time.

At the airport, Dad invited me back for Christmas. And we hugged.

I'm grateful for small blessings.

The land below me, the land of my ancestors, has puddles of lakes, vast brownish-green forests and is surrounded by salt water. The cold Atlantic Ocean encases us, but is not our prison. They came from France and Ireland and England, my people, hundreds of years ago. Some came from Nova Scotia, crossing on boats and ice floes to hunt and fish and were maybe even hired by Whites to hunt the Beothuck Indians, our extinct Newfoundland people. We don't know for sure. Some of my people have probably lived here for not hundreds but thousands of years.

A humbling thought.

I carry their genes in me and I embrace their yarns. I carry the marks of this *New-found-land* on my physical body and in my heart, mind and soul.

She's in me and her people, too, as are Poppy Murphy's.

I'm who I am.

Je suis qui je suis.

I'm them.

They're me.

Jackytar

The way God made me.

I don't blame or judge anyone. Not even myself. But what I can do is try to understand, to forgive and love again more fully. I want to give myself over to love. I'm not who I was last week. I'm not who I was yesterday or this morning and I won't be the same person later this evening when I embrace Keith.

I know I have my work cut out for me. There's no time to lose. We need to talk. Really and truly talk. There'll be much soul searching and hard work cut out for the both of us, especially if Keith is to go into rehab and we are to survive as a couple.

Love is all that matters.

I am *Alexandre Murphy*. Jackytar. Newfoundlander. Educator. Brother. Son. Fighter. Survivor. Lover.

And I have many silences yet to break.

Still.

References

Batstone, B. *The Mysterious Mummer and other Newfoundland Stories*. St. John's, NL: Jesperson Press, 1984.

Charbonneau, P. & L. Barrette. *Contre vents et marées, l'histoire des francophones de Terre-Neuve et du Labrador*. Moncton, Nouveau Brunswick: Les Éditions d'Acadie, 1992.

Duncan, N. "The Outports." In R. Goulding Ed., *Passages, Literature of Newfoundland and Labrador* (Vol. 3, pp. 68-71). St. John's, NL: Breakwater Books Limited, 1980.

Fitzgerald, J. Newfoundland Fireside Stories. St. John's, Newfoundland: Creative Publishers, 1990.

Hawkes, B. Building Bridges. Toronto: Metropolitan Community Church of Toronto, 2003a.

Hawkes, B. Leadership and Courage. Toronto: Metropolitan Community Church of Toronto, 2003b.

Hawkes, B. Spirituality and Faith. Toronto: Metropolitan Community Church of Toronto, 2003c.

Hawkes, B. Ya Ya Sisterhood: We are only as Sick as our Secrets. Toronto: Metropolitan Community Church of Toronto, 2004.

Lowell, R. *The New Priest in Conception Bay*. Toronto: McClelland and Stewart, 1974.

Newhook, C. "Jennies." In Mostly in Rodneys (pp. 89-91). St. John's: Creative Printers & Publishers Limited, 1985.

Story, G.M. *A Newfoundland Dialect Questionnaire, Avalon Peninsula*. St. John's: Memorial University of Newfoundland, 1959.

Story, G.M. "The Dialects of Newfoundland English." In H.J. Paddock (Ed.), *Languages in Newfoundland and Labrador* (Preliminary ed., pp. 74-80). St. John's: Memorial University, Dept. of Linguistics, 1977.

Story, G.M., W.J. Kirwin, & J.D.A. Widdowson, *Dictionary of Newfoundland English* (2nd ed.). Toronto: University of Toronto Press, 1990.

Acknowledgements

I am extremely grateful to my editor, Tamara Reynish, my publisher, Rebecca Rose, my designer, Rhonda Molloy, Karla Hayward at Jesperson Publishing, and my mentor, Ardra Cole. Early reads by Gary Knowles, Peter Trifonas, Rinaldo Walcott, André Grace, Verna and Edgar Gosse, Ryan Jackson, and L. Hargrove were invaluable. My genius friend and irrepressible accomplice in many deeds, Ed Piotrowski, did a thorough and entertaining last read. I thank Rev. Dr. Brent Hawkes for his inspiration. I am extremely thankful for the Social Sciences and Humanities Research Council of Canada, which partially funded the research leading to this novel.

ED PIOTROWSKI

d ouglas Gosse has a doctorate in Social Justice &
Cultural Studies and works in the Faculty of Education
at Nipissing University, North Bay, Ontario. He earned
several prestigious awards for the research leading to
jackytar. Many readers have enjoyed his other two
novels, *The Celtic Cross* and the *Romeo & Juliet Murders*.
Douglas Gosse may be reached at douglasg@nipissingu.ca

■